The SACRED PORCH

Dr. Azita Khashayar

CHAPTER ONE

As Edward was walking out of his office on Friday looking forward to the weekend at home, he remembered that his boss wanted to see him before he left work. Burned out from a day of entering insurance applications from new clients into his computer, he impatiently turned toward his boss's office. He walked through the open door hesitantly, not knowing if he was interrupting.

"Ed! Come on in and have a seat." Gregg smiled and offered the very bright red chair in front of his desk. Edward couldn't help wonder why anyone would pay money to look at this bright red chair every day. "Ed, I have good news and bad news. Are you ready?"

Edward wasn't quite ready for this question, reacting with a long stare. "OK, Ed, I'll give you the good news first. You're going to have a very long vacation with no pay; but the bad news is that you have to come back to this boring job of yours and continue working with us for a long time."

Edward couldn't quite comprehend what "a very long vacation" meant and why that was the good news. He knew that the economy was bad and a lot of people were losing their jobs. He remembered reading about the world economy changing for the worse. But he never thought that he could be one of the unfortunates who would be searching for a new job.

Gregg continued, "I'm sure you're aware of what's going on in this current economy. Times are tough; we've been hit by this recession harder than we'd anticipated." Edward began to feel a little numb and dizzy. Staring at Gregg, he vaguely caught "bad economy...don't think of this as a layoff...try to think of this as an unpaid vacation." It all dissolved for him into "yak yak yak blah blah blah"..."when the economy heals we can find a space for you...yak yak yak blah blah blah." Edward was numb.

"I don't understand," Edward replied quietly and submissively. "I have been working for you for years, and I don't need a vacation. I'm very happy here. My numbers haven't dropped, and I'm always on time."

"That is exactly why I want you back as soon as I can afford you. You're a young man, Ed, and when I was your age...blah blah blah yak yak yak. I am truly sorry."

Edward couldn't think straight. He couldn't figure out if he was fired or laid off or being given a real vacation. "Gregg, do you have any idea when you'll hire me back?" Edward asked with a trembling voice.

"No clue, but I'll let you know as soon as I know. Times are hard; if you can just do some odd jobs for a while we'll see where we are." Then on a more personal note Gregg added, "And tell your sweet fiancée that I said hi and that I haven't forgotten her parents' dinner invitation. I'll call and set up some time to see them as soon as I have some extra time. Good luck to you, I'm sure we'll be talking soon…blah blah blah yak yak yak. Let me know if you need anything."

Like a survivor of a train wreck, Edward walked out feeling dizzy, unsure of what had happened to him.

He had forgotten about his fiancée. How was Lily going to react to this news? He felt simultaneously angry and helpless. How could he explain this to her? He couldn't call her. He had to see her and talk with her. *Everything will be OK,* he thought as he drove to his apartment. He began an internal inventory, glad that he had saved up some money for a rainy day. He owned the apartment that his mother had left him when she died. At least he wouldn't be too worried financially for a while. But what was he supposed to do with himself? Where was he going to look for a job? Was he even going to look for a job?

And again, Lily…he started worrying about Lily's reaction. Lily had made it clear that she was counting on him to keep her happy and living in the lifestyle that they'd chosen. He had promised her that. What was she going to think of him now? He felt crushed.

When he got home, Edward called Lily and told her that they needed to talk, suggesting she come over to his place. As he was sitting in front of the television randomly changing channels, his mind wondered at the way this day had turned out. At least he had Lily to talk this through with. Everything was going to be OK. He kept thinking how to break this to her with a minimum of drama. And what about the wedding? She was in the throes of wedding plans, anticipating a very special time that this news could ruin. Edward was "what-iffing" himself into a lather.

Click, the door opened. Lily walked in and dropped her keys into the bowl by the front door. She came into the living room, leaned over, and kissed him on the head. "What's up? You sounded absolutely frazzled on the phone."

Edward noticed that she was dressed for what looked like a cocktail party—hair up, makeup on—and remembered what he had found so attractive about her when they met. But now her bright red lipstick reminded him of the garish red chair in his boss's office.

"I can't wait to tell you about my day...wonderful," Lily excitedly began. Lily was a very tall, slender woman with curly red locks, large hazel eyes that noted everything and everyone in her path, and a face that seemed to smile at it all. Now her good cheer made him squirm. She had seen the most beautiful wedding dress after setting her mind on another one and now couldn't make up her mind which to choose. She went on about a meeting she had in a few hours with a wedding planner who was usually booked for about two years ahead of time, but who they were so lucky to get only because her stepmother knew someone that knew the planner well enough to ask for this favor. Lily went on and on before she finished.

Edward anxiously listened to her without saying a word. He tried to smile, telling her that he was sure she would be beautiful in whatever dress she chose and that, yes, it was fabulous that they had snared such a sought-after wedding planner. Though his anxiety mounted with every word, Lily's long report also felt like a reprieve from having to tell her the bad news. So when she finally asked him what it was that he wanted to talk to her about, he felt suddenly confronted by his executioner.

Take a deep breath, Edward said to himself and finally began to tell her about his day. "You'd better sit down, Lil. I've got a major tale of woe."

When she heard he had lost his job, a look of utter shock crept over Lily's face and she asked Edward what he had done that got him fired. Edward kept telling her that he did nothing and that his boss had accused him of nothing. He was given this "long vacation," as his boss explained, because the economy was going through a rough patch and that he was to be taken back as soon as everything was more stable.

Lily was clearly disappointed. She was starting to look annoyed and told Ed that she couldn't believe how he "just accepted this decision so passively" instead of insisting that Gregg find someone else to "cut loose." She accused Edward of acting selfishly. After all, there were their plans, their wedding, and their future together, not to mention the expense of setting up a new household...blah blah blah yak yak yak. She insisted that Edward's situation had nothing to do with the economy, that people were responsible for losing their jobs, not the economy.

"But honey, I always think about our future. You don't mean what you're saying. Gregg didn't give me a chance. He'd already made up his mind. There was nothing I could've done."

Lily had heard enough and got up to go to her appointment with the wedding planner. As she picked up her purse from the table, she asked if her tears had ruined her makeup. "Your makeup is perfect, Lily, have a good time," Edward replied. Lily hurried out of the apartment, increasingly annoyed at Edward for not standing up for himself to keep his job.

Edward couldn't understand how Lily could just go on with her meeting with the wedding planner while he was suffering the loss of his job. He was hurt that she didn't stay with him when he needed her. He dimly knew that there was something wrong with the way she had responded to his news, so he defensively reviewed the events of the day, assuring himself that there was no way he could have reversed Gregg's decision to let him go.

Numbed, Edward sat in front of the television for what seemed like hours, feeling terrible about not convincing Greg to keep his job. He was thirty-five years old with no plan for his future, thirty-five and starting all over. Perhaps he had taken his job for granted and now had to pay God back for not appreciating all of his blessings. Wow, was he becoming his grandmother and thinking about God? His grandmother always used to say, "Eddie, you have to appreciate all of your blessings or God can just take them away!" This is a mean God, he'd always thought. But now, with his uncertain future, he shouldn't even think about what he felt for God, so he wouldn't get God mad!

Startled by his cell phone's ring, he impatiently searched for it around the couch. "Hello, Edward, this is Lucy. Do you have a minute?" Lily's stepmother, Lucy, rarely called Edward directly. Anytime she wanted them over for dinner or something, she usually just arranged it with Lily.

"Yes, Lucy, how are you?"

"Well, Edward, we heard that you lost your job and don't show much drive to get it back. I'm so sorry, Edward, but Lily is heartbroken and she doesn't want you to contact her for a while. Please understand that this is a very hard time for her too. She's confused and is taking this very hard."

Edward couldn't believe his ears. Was this really happening? In one day he had been temporarily laid off, perhaps even permanently fired, and then given a temporary, perhaps even a permanent, time-out by his fiancée. "Lucy, please let me explain. There must be a misunderstanding. This situation just happened today. I couldn't have prevented it. I haven't even had time to think this out, much less move forward. Lily's way overreacting. Let me come over and I'll talk it over with Lily. Everything will be all OK, I promise."

"I'm sorry, Edward, I don't think you understood me. Lily doesn't want to talk to you. She won't see you. Maybe if you spoke to Gregg in the morning and got your job back first, things would be different. That would make everything better for both of you. I've gotta go. Really try to get that position back, Lily is counting on it." Lucy hung up without saying good-bye.

Edward couldn't believe what he had just heard. Lily had left to meet the wedding planner. When did she have time to talk to Lucy, let alone make such an important decision? Even more bewildering, how could she do it without even discussing it with him? Edward hadn't even argued with Lily, wishing her well on her way out. He decided to call and talk her out of this silly idea. His call went straight to voice mail. So did several others. Finally he left a message for her to call him back, adding that she was being silly, because he loved her very much. He told himself that this was a huge misunderstanding that caused Lily to overreact, given the stress of wedding preparations, and that everything would be OK.

CHAPTER TWO

Edward hadn't left his apartment for four days. He'd been surviving on potato chips and Coke, cold pizza and beer, watching reruns of reruns. He was working himself into a first-class depression. During all this time, he thought about taking a shower, if only to kill time until Lily got over her tantrum and agreed to talk. But he couldn't summon the will to do even that. He managed to leave a few messages with Gregg's secretary, but got no response. He called Lucy a few times, but she wasn't answering either. He kept checking his cell phone to make sure that it was working.

There was a knock on the door. Startled, he jumped up and opened the door, hoping Lily would appear on the other side. But there was only a postman with a small package. "Are you

Mr. Edward Evans? I have a package for you." Edward nodded, signed his name, took the parcel, closed the door, and stared at the box. He couldn't believe this. Special delivery? A signature? Things seemed to be going from bad to worse.

Edward opened the package, which contained a letter in Lily's handwriting.

Ed, it is very difficult for me to write to you, but I have no choice. I want to return your ring, since it was your mother's and it must mean a lot to you. You have to understand that everything between us is over. It wasn't just you losing your job, but much more. I feel that we are no longer compatible. I cannot believe that you are the same man that I thought I loved. You have changed so much. Here I was trying to plan the most important day of our life (our wedding) and you tell me that you lost your job and there is nothing that you can do about it. What did you expect me to do? I thought you were better than that. You didn't appreciate the fact that I was able to find the best wedding planner around here and had a chance to meet with her. You didn't even offer to meet her with me. What happened to all of your feelings for me? I thought you really cared. But now I see that all you really care about is yourself. You couldn't care less if we don't even have a big beautiful wedding.

Obviously we want different things from life. I have big dreams and you don't. I want much more from life and you can't make up your mind about anything. Sorry for the way things worked out, but I had to be honest. Don't call me anymore. Keep Lucy out of this. Take care of yourself. I will always remember the good times we shared.

Sincerely,
Lily

Edward took his mother's ring at the bottom of the box and put it in his pocket. He placed the opened package on the coffee table, sat on his sofa, covered his face in his hands, and wept. He must have gone on for a while, shaken by his own loud sobbing. It seemed like crying for the loss of his mother all over again, feeling helpless and small. How dare Lily believe that he had no big dreams? His mother always said that he was a special boy. She always encouraged him to follow his heart. She always sat quietly listening to his dreams. Since he was the only child, his mother had a lot of special time to spend with him. What would his mother say to him now if she were alive? How did little Edward, with such high hopes, become this thirty-five-year-old who didn't know what to do with himself? He had done everything that he was supposed to do, and still it wasn't enough. His mother used to say that life just happens sometimes, when one shouldn't give up but start walking a different path. He tried to imagine what his mother would tell him in this situation. Was this one of those times? What new direction might she point him toward? He couldn't come up with anything helpful.

More days passed with Edward not feeling like doing anything. He had some weird dreams about little angels flying all around his apartment, but he couldn't make any sense of what they were trying to do. The only good thing was that he didn't dream about Lily, so that he at least avoided that pain while asleep.

Early one morning Edward decided that he needed some strong coffee. He looked in the mirror, grimacing when he saw that he hadn't shaved for days and looked awful. He couldn't care less, telling himself that he just needed coffee and a little fresh air. As he opened his apartment door, he glimpsed a boy of seven or eight in the hallway. The boy walked toward him and asked if he would please buy a newspaper and some homemade cookies.

Edward gave him a five-dollar bill, grabbed a newspaper, picked one cookie from the open jar, and without saying a word left the building. He found the cookie tasty, perhaps simply because he was sick of eating chips and Coke.

The coffee shop close to his apartment was owned by a fellow named Gary. Gary was a pretty cool guy, older, maybe fifty, but OK nonetheless. He would usually come out on the floor and greet his regular customers. He made the best coffee drinks but had no clue what to serve with them. Some of his customers were known to bring their own pastries.

When Edward arrived at the coffee shop, he greeted Gary, grabbed a hot cup of black coffee, found a corner table, and sat down. He began reading some headlines from the newspaper he had bought from the boy in his building. As he scanned the want ads, an odd advertisement caught his eye: "Handyman needed to redo an old porch. Room and board provided. Live near lake with views. Pays well for applicant with clean background check and good manners." It occurred to Edward that leaving his apartment would help him forget about everything for a while. Maybe he needed the peace and quiet of a new place in order to relax and find a solution to getting Lily back. He never doubted that he had to get her back.

Edward called the number in the ad. He provided the requested information and volunteered that he was ready to start work tomorrow. *What do I have to lose?* he thought. He used to redo porches with his father when he was growing up. A very hard worker, his father always let Edward help with remodeling jobs. "Good training," he'd say. *So let's do this together, Dad,* he now thought to himself.

Having decided to make this move, Edward took a few hours to call friends who had left him messages to tell them that he was going away for a while and would be in touch when he returned. There wasn't much more to say, since they already knew what had happened. Lily had spread the word. This would be a good move. Get out of the city and do some manual labor to shake out the cobwebs. Yes, this would be good.

His cell phone rang. "Mr. Evans?"

"Yes, this is Edward Evans."

The voice on the other end was that of an old man, maybe in his eighties. "I need you to start my handy work as soon as possible, please. I will discuss everything with you when you arrive. I am calling to give you my address, son."

It had been a long time since Edward had heard anyone call him son.

This poor man sounded so sincere. He couldn't have done a background check, since Edward had applied for this job about an hour earlier. Edward learned that the man lived in a town named Little Falls, which was over two hundred miles to the north. Good, the farther away the better. He arranged to start the next morning, happy to escape his apartment and all of his drama for a while. He had inherited the apartment from his mother, but the place was never quite the same without her. He had thoughts of selling it; but at the end of the day he couldn't detach from his mother's memory so easily.

On the road, he understood how his father must have felt going to someone's home for a remodel. As Edward remembered, it was an exciting adventure. But now that he was a grown man, this was just another job. He hoped the change of scenery would lift his spirits. There was something invigorating about this new venture as a handyman. Lots of people with advanced degrees were working as handymen, book clerks, baristas, and at other menial jobs these days. He felt no stigma in that. Indeed, it took him away from his routine, and the prospect of using his hands made him feel alive again.

As he approached his destination, there were fewer and fewer homes in sight. He had never heard of Little Falls before, and the increasingly unpopulated landscape explained why. One good thing about this job was that there would be no one to ask him anything, no familiar faces, no one except a bent-over old rube who was probably not very mentally alert. He might have Alzheimer's in addition to being an uneducated rustic. He seemed naively trusting. *What if I were a crazy man whom this poor, isolated old man is letting into his home?*

As he approached the driveway, he couldn't believe his eyes. This little house, surrounded by a protective thicket of trees, looked over a hundred years old. The roof looked as if it couldn't weather the slightest storm. He was surprised the house was standing. Why would anyone pay good money to fix an old porch for a house that winds could sweep away before the work was even finished? On the other hand, as he looked over the landscape he noticed that the flowers and plants were mostly native, along with various grasses that seemed to have never been trimmed. The house itself had an emerald-green door that matched the trees perfectly. In spite of its fragility, he saw a home at one with its surroundings. He felt at peace there.

"Hello! Anybody home?" Edward hollered. There was no answer. He walked toward the front door and saw where the wood on the front porch was very unstable. "Hello, sir? Are you in here? I am here to fix your porch." But there was no answer. All Edward could hear was the sound of the wind moving the large tree branches. He went back to his car, opened the trunk, and began to unload his tools. He was happy to be using them again. His father always took pride in them, and Edward used to think they were magical. Every time little Edward thought a remodeling job was impossible to accomplish, his father would remind him to trust these tools. Even after his father's passing about ten years ago, they looked as good as new. He had helped his father fix many porches, so he was fairly comfortable working wood.

As he unloaded the tool boxes from the car and placed them near the porch, he glanced at his own image in the side mirror. He hadn't shaved for many days now, and his beard was growing quite long. He could also use a haircut. "This poor old man is going to be afraid of me," he chuckled to himself. He felt good about looking a little tough. "Maybe I'll just keep my hair and beard long for now. It might scare the old man a little and he'll leave me alone."

Edward sat on one of four steps that reached the porch. His mind drifted to Lily. Suddenly feeling sad and lonely, he hid his face inside his palms and imagined meeting Lily for the first time. How could events in one single day change so much in his life? He couldn't believe that the life he had imagined with Lily was over. Why had she been so dressed up just to meet one of her friends? In the year they were dating, Lily almost always dressed casually. She hated dressing every day for her bank job, so she would dress down any chance she could.

"Hi there, son. I have some lemonade and fresh eggs for us to start the day." An old man's voice surprised him and he quickly stood up. "Good morning, sir," Edward replied automatically. The old man's appearance wasn't what Edward expected. He was a tall, lean, and physically strong black man with a very manly voice. He had a clean-shaven face and was wearing khaki pants, a clean white shirt, and a pair of white tennis shoes.

"You must be shocked. When I spoke with you I was fighting a mean case of laryngitis, and thanks to my neighbor's chicken soup, I'm as good as new." The man offered his hand and said,

"I'm Max, son. Breakfast is ready, so if you want to wash up, the door is open."

Edward was unsure of his decision to take this job. This man clearly wasn't that old, and he clearly wasn't intimidated by Edward's tough appearance. Edward tried to figure out Max's age. He had some wrinkles, but not enough to categorize him as a senior citizen. His hair was silver, but then again, he had a friend in college who went gray at twenty. As Edward walked inside the old house he was impressed by how clean it was. There was a small kitchen on the left that had a large window overlooking some greenery. To the right of the door was a small room with an old brown leather couch and a small coffee table. He didn't see a television. There were some stairs in front of the door that Edward figured went up to some bedrooms. He finally noticed the bathroom door to the side of the stairway.

Cleaned up, Edward entered the kitchen to the smell of fried eggs. He walked toward the kitchen table and sat down on one of the four empty chairs. Max placed two china plates and two silver forks on the table. The men ate their breakfast in complete silence. Edward was filled with many questions about Max's life, what he did for a living foremost among them. For now, more practical concerns replaced them. He was hoping that he didn't have to sleep on the leather couch, but felt guilty about letting Max sleep there. "Sir, does this place have two bedrooms?"

"Yes, son," Max answered.

"My name is Edward, sir, not son." He regretted his comment as soon as it was out of his mouth.

"My name isn't sir either, son. But you can call me that if you wish. I'm used to it. It reminds me of my years in the army. So many young men used to call me sir. I was a major back in those days. Some people were so nervous they called me Sir Major." By this time both men were laughing.

"Yes sir, Sir Major." Edward couldn't remember the last time he laughed so carelessly and comfortably. He felt as if he was where he belonged. Even though this job didn't make sense to him, he knew he was meant to be there. He couldn't help but think how angry Lily would be if she knew what he was doing. He missed Lily. He kept checking his cell phone to see if he had missed any calls from her. He decided to just stop thinking and work on the porch.

"Sir Major, let's talk about your porch." The men walked outside and discussed the remodeling step by step. This was a big job. Edward didn't ask Max anything about money. He didn't care about the payment. He was having a very interesting time, and he didn't want it to end. He felt content.

In the evening when they were sitting on the couch and relaxing, Edward asked Max what he thought of his appearance when he first saw him. "I thought you must love Jesus, son. You look so much like him, being a carpenter and all, with all that hair." The men had a good laugh. That night Edward was too tired to think about Lily. He decided that he would think about her tomorrow. He dreamt about five or six little angels flying around his bed in the little house. In his dream Max was sitting on his couch and laughing with the angels. He could see that the angels were jumping up and down in front of Max to entertain him and play with him. Max played with them like a child. He would run after them and laugh with them. What an interesting man this Max is, Edward thought in his dream.

CHAPTER THREE

The next morning Edward woke up to the smell of fresh coffee. He couldn't remember the last time he woke up to that smell. For a long time he had started his day with a walk to a coffee shop to get his morning fix. Max had left a note on the kitchen table for him: "Enjoy the coffee, there's sausage on the stove. I'm off for my morning walk." The sausage was perfect. He would never have chosen sausage and coffee for breakfast, but Max had his way of doing things and Edward didn't mind being served this way.

He walked outside to the porch to plan his day and decided to remove the old wood one small section at a time, replacing it with the new wood as he went along. It took several hours before he had removed the first section of rotten wood. He was sitting on

the steps to rest when he noticed Max walking toward him holding what seemed to be a rather large brown box. "Do you need my
help, sir?"

"No, son, I can manage," Max answered. He explained that his
lovely neighbor had given them some ham sandwiches along with
some fruit and vegetables from her garden. Edward wondered
how far away this neighbor lived. Max must have walked a long
way. The spring sun was making the day very hot, but the thought
of ham sandwiches made everything more bearable. As the men
were sitting together eating, they didn't speak. Edward was thinking about his work. He didn't care how long this job was going to
take. For it turned out that taking this "long vacation" was good
news after all.

After lunch Max went inside the house to rest. It took the rest
of the day for Edward to finish the corner side of the porch. The
next day Edward decided to start fixing the railings. He noticed
that the railings weren't really damaged but simply needed a thor-
ough sanding and painting. It took most of the afternoon to sand
half of the railings. The repetitive motion of sanding was like med-
itation for Edward.

After Max arose from his nap, he called Edward to have some
lemonade inside, where it was cooler. Again the men sat together
in complete silence. Edward took a long time to finish his drink,
perhaps because he was tired and needed more rest.

"There must be a good reason that a young man like you wants
to get away from his life," Max offered.

Edward didn't know how to respond. He wondered why Max
concluded that he needed to get away. But as much as he wanted
to get away from everyone, he felt a need to talk to someone who
could understand him. "Well, there were two good reasons, sir. I
was given a very long vacation from my job, and my fiancée left

me," Edward replied. And without saying another word, he continued drinking his lemonade.

Max leaned forward toward Edward, as if he was going to share a secret with him. "I lost my wife of forty-five years a few years ago. We were good for each other. I know how it feels to lose someone you love." Edward told Max that he was sorry for his loss. He added that he couldn't imagine how it felt to lose someone after so many years of living together. "We weren't just living together. We were best friends. I lost my best friend for a while." Edward looked puzzled by Max's last remark. Max continued, "I will join her again. We are separate only for a while. It will be a joyous reunion. Don't get me wrong, I'm not sitting here waiting to die to join my wife. I am going to live my life full circle. Later, whenever my time comes, then I'll find out what she already knows. Isn't that exciting, son?"

Edward had never thought about death in that way. Suddenly he was excited by how he would feel to see his mother again, which in turn evoked the same thought about his father. "But how can you be sure that we're going to meet our loved ones when we die?"

Max didn't answer right away. He stood up and walked toward the coffee table by the couch. He picked up a wooden box from under the coffee table and brought it back to the kitchen table. He opened the box and showed Edward a black-and-white picture of a young woman. She had long dark hair, tan skin, and a smile that would brighten anyone's day. She was quite beautiful. Max looked at Edward and said, "I don't know where she is now, but I know that she still exists. I don't have any concrete answer about her existence, but I feel her close to my heart. I lived with this woman for a very long time. She knew what I wanted to say before I said it. And now I believe that we'll meet again someday. Don't you think that I'm going to meet her again, son?"

"Yes sir, you will," Edward replied. "Where was your wife from?"

"Her parents were from Brazil and she was born in the States. We met in front of a supermarket. I had bought more groceries than I could handle. I must have spilled more than four bags of fruit all over the parking lot and she helped me gather them all up. She teasingly suggested that I use the grocery cart next time." The men started to laugh together. Edward felt very close to Max. Suddenly the loss of Lily didn't seem as big. He wasn't sure if he could call Lily his best friend.

"Well, I don't know what to say to you. But I'm sorry I made you remember," Edward said.

"You didn't make me remember anything," Max replied. "I never forgot my wife, son. I just wanted to share a part of my life story with you. If you have a solid, two-way relationship with your life partner, then she won't leave you. Think of your relationship as a circle. Yours wasn't complete. That is why it slipped away. In life everything is like a full circle. Too many cracks and leaks will eventually dissolve any bond, big or small."

Edward knew what Max meant. He was right. His job had many cracks. He was never happy to go to work. He went there to pay his bills. He had no real passion for it. His relationship with Lily had cracks too. He could never be himself with Lily; she was far too criticizing. His circles weren't complete in the way Max had described. He began to realize that something was missing from the way he related to everything.

"I understand what you mean by complete circles, sir. But how do you know when your circle is complete?" Edward asked.

"How do you feel about working here, son? I mean at this moment and from the moment you picked up the phone and called for this job?"

Edward realized that everything felt right, but he didn't know why. He had to think about this for a while. With a rush of gratitude, he knew that Max was going to give him all the time he needed to arrive at an answer. "I'm not sure how to explain it. I just knew that I had to call your number and that I had to come here. I felt sure about it. I had no idea if I was sane for making a decision like this, you know? I mean, I went to college to do a different kind of job. While I was growing up I learned how to do this porch work from helping my dad, but it didn't make sense to me. It didn't resonate, didn't have meaning for me. But now it feels right to be here. It feels right to talk to you."

Edward was amazed how quickly he had opened up to this man. He barely knew him, but he felt a bond between them.

"Do you think your circle is complete at where you are right now in your life, son?"

"I'm not sure I understand you, sir. Even if something is good and feels right, bad things can happen too. Then how do you know if you are in a complete circle with someone or not?" Edward asked.

Max walked closer and answered, "You're right about that. Life happens in any path that you take. But if you're where you have to be, then there is no nagging voice inside wishing you were somewhere else. You get lost in your moments so you don't have to live with the little voice that keeps complaining. That is the voice of intuition. We all have it. A lot of times we choose to ignore it, but it won't leave us. This voice stays with us throughout our lives. If we are in a complete circle in our relationships—whether with people, our activity, or anything around us—it stays quiet and content. But if we are in a wrong place, for example, or in a wrong relationship that can harm us and hurt us, the voice will keep talking. Even though we mightn't be listening, intuition doesn't judge. Have you ever experienced this?'

Edward nodded. He knew the voice that Max was talking about. He remembered not being happy at his job. He kept hearing the nagging voice that kept telling him that he was wasting his life. But he didn't have the courage to leave. What kept stopping him from listening to his intuition? Maybe it was fear. Fear of the unknown. He had to fulfill his role as a man in society. He had obligations and responsibilities that tied him to the job that he didn't like. How could he just listen to that voice and let go of everything? Edward asked Max if he thought it was possible to have stayed in his old job because of self-imposed responsibilities if he had listened to his inner voice. Max explained that he could have kept the job and still searched for what he liked. But he should never ignore his dreams. Max said that he believed that every person comes to life to fulfill a purpose, and he should never abandon that. The only way to true happiness according to Max was to live in purpose. He thanked Max for the lemonade, and he got up to continue with the railings.

As Edward was sanding the rest of the railings, he tried to imagine how his circle was becoming complete with each wooden railing. It must feel good for the railings too, he thought.

CHAPTER FOUR

Edward worked hard over the next few days, finishing almost one half of the porch. It was early afternoon, and he had removed most of the wood in the remaining section. He decided to remove a few more pieces before starting to rebuild. As he grasped one with his left hand, he felt something that seemed to have been nailed to the wood from underneath. He carefully removed the board and cautiously turned it around to see what was placed underneath it. He saw a book-sized container wrapped in some rotten-looking piece of black leather that was nailed to the wood. He immediately called Max. "Sir Major, you need to come here."

Max stepped outside, his face filled with curiosity. Both men were surprised, not sure what they had found. Max asked Edward to bring the wood over to him so they could find out what was inside. Sitting down together on the steps, Edward asked Max what he thought this could be. "Whatever it is inside, I guess it's time to open it," Max replied.

Edward carefully pulled the small nails from the old, rotten wood. As the package released from the wood, it opened up. Inside there was more leather wrapping, which firmly covered a rectangular metal box, which was easily opened. There inside they saw pages and pages of handwritten letters that were neatly stacked together. All of them began with "Dear God."

Eager to read the letters, Edward asked Max if they could look at them now or wait until he finished his day's work on the porch. "Plans change, son. Let's go wash our hands and start reading them. These letters were meant to be found by you, so you will get the pleasure of reading them out loud." After Edward washed up, he found Max calmly waiting for him with the letters stacked on the kitchen table. He sat down on one of the chairs facing Max.

The letters were written neatly and legibly in dark black ink on thin beige papers that looked old and worn out. Edward began reading in a clear and calm voice.

Dear God,

You are probably shocked that I am contacting you by writing a letter. I will explain. I wasn't sure if my grammar was good enough to write, but finally I decided that you will forgive my mistakes. People say different things about how we are supposed to contact you, but I'm not sure if I believe them. I decided that I am going to do it my way. There is a strong desire in me to write some letters to you. I have had these desires for many years now. I just couldn't bring myself to do anything about them. Finally my desires won.

I just couldn't get rid of them. It is like a nagging voice in my heart that I can't quiet down. So here I am writing my first letter to you. But I do have a few requests for you. I want to write them down to make everything very clear so there is no misunderstanding between us.

First of all, please don't let my husband and family ever see this letter and/or anything else that I will write to you from now on. He isn't a bad person, but these aren't for his eyes. My wish is that you will let someone who is very special to you find them, someone whose heart is as pure as the clear waters. I will do my part to be very discreet about them. I promise to hide them in a very safe place where I have no control over who will find them. I know that you will do your part and make sure someone that you know is right will find and read them. My desire ever since I can remember has been to write a book. You know what lengths I go through to find and borrow books anytime that I can. I know that my husband Paul doesn't appreciate me reading books.

I think he blames me for not being able to give him any children. I don't blame him for not having any. Sometimes in my secret thoughts I think maybe a man can also have some problems too. But soon I try to change my thoughts. Please forgive me for them, since I cannot control them. Paul is clearly very disappointed in me. I think that is why he always comes home very late. He is a good man, I know. I have prayed so much to you, God, to be able to bear a child. Sometimes I have even blamed you for making me barren. I'm not sure why this is happening to me, but I know that it must be your will. Paul doesn't want to talk about anything that relates to children. This makes me feel sad and lonely. I'm glad I can talk to you about all this. Thanks for listening to me.

I asked Paul to take me to my parents' home and divorce me so he could remarry and have children of his own. But he says we shouldn't talk about sinful things. He is a firm believer in you. But I think you are more understanding and more flexible than most people think. Although it has been many years that I have been asking you to give me a child, I want you to know that I accept your will. I will live my life this way. But I want to write my story. I know wanting to be an author is asking the impossible of my life. But with you, everything is possible. Sometimes I think if I write my life experiences, who is going to find them extraordinary? An old woman in her forties should just do what she does best and keep her house and her husband. But there is a desire in me, God, that I don't understand. I have desire to place all these thoughts on the paper. Here is my first writing to you. I hope you like it.

Inside the core of my flesh,
Within the inner world of life,
Within color, within light, is a pause.
The voice, the space, the force,
I feel in the quietness a presence,
My presence or a presence,
Where life flows, rises, falls, changes, dances, expands, shines, twinkles, awakes, spins, creates, forms, reforms, unites and loves.
In it I breathe, in awe I am free.
I know that I already told you, but keep this and all of the upcoming letters to yourself, at least while I am alive. Hopefully I will see who you find special enough to discover my writings.

With Love and Respect,
Sara

Max's face was calm as Edward finished the first letter to God. "When do you think she lived here?" Edward asked.

"I cannot be sure, but I bought this place around thirty-five years ago. My wife and I used to come here for vacations. She liked the peace and quiet." Max's eyes were filled with tears as he got up to drink a glass of water. "You see, son," he continued, "we never had any children. I always wondered how noisy and busy this place would have been if we had a few kids to play around here. But I guess that wasn't part of my lessons."

Edward didn't understand why a kind and loving God chose such difficult lessons for his people. "This doesn't sound like a very nice God," Edward said out loud.

"Well, son, apparently this God loved Sara enough that he kept his end of the bargain, and he didn't let anyone find her letters until now. This obviously makes you the very special person that Sara wished for and God chose."

Edward couldn't comprehend how God could have so much faith in him. He wasn't even sure if God was right. Maybe mistakes happen even as far as the heavens are concerned. He thought about Sara and her dreams. How silly she was to believe that God was listening to her thoughts and that he would find a very special person to find her letters. He found it ironic that God had chosen him, which only proved that the discovery was an accident. It was good that Sara was no longer alive, since she would be very disappointed to see who found her letters.

"I'm not so sure that I have the pure-as-the-waters heart that Sara was talking about. If God had his little angels pick me, then they must be very new at this. Why didn't this God just help this woman Sara publish her writings? Why leave them buried in here forever?"

Max thought about Edward's questions for a minute and said, "First of all, now you found them, so they weren't buried forever. Secondly, you found them, so you can publish them for her.

Remember, you are part of some special plan. So you better hold your end of the bargain."

Edward couldn't understand what Max was talking about. Why was he trying to make up stories about God's special plan? If he knew Edward better, he would question God's special plan. However, there was no reason to argue with him about this. God or no God, plan or no plan, Edward still found it interesting that this woman had written some letters to God that he looked forward to reading.

Max and Edward agreed to continue reading Sara's letters one by one between Edward's work on the porch. That evening, they decided to read the next letter before they slept.

Edward began.

Dear God,

Sorry I haven't written for so long. But you know the terrible situation that we were faced with. I had to write this letter to you, because I had to thank you for saving our lives. I couldn't have imagined this could happen to us. I am so glad that I decided to keep our dog, Joe. Even though Paul kept nagging me not to keep him because he might have some kind of disease, I didn't listen to him. Joe's face was so desperate and sad, his eyes so beautiful and innocent, when I first spotted him in front of the house looking for food. Yet Paul resisted keeping him. I kept repeating how nice it would be to help this poor dog. But only when I started to cry, for what must have been for a long time, did Paul relent. He knew that he had to let me keep Joe if he didn't want me to nag him day and night. Then I cried with happiness, though I had no idea what a prize Joe would turn out to be.

I'm not sure if you purposely had that rattlesnake come around here, but it was very scary. In less than a few seconds I could have lost my husband if Joe hadn't jumped and caught the snake's neck. I still cannot write without shaking when I recall that horrific scene. I was cleaning the kitchen floor and Paul was standing in front of the open door, with Joe standing calmly next to him. Suddenly Joe jumped past Paul and caught the snake with his teeth around the snake's neck. Paul was shocked, not seeing the snake until Joe attacked it. I didn't have time to move or see anything. Paul grabbed his rifle and finished the snake off. Then he knelt kissing Joe admiringly and gratefully. God, I thank you for saving Joe. I thank you for saving Paul. Paul says that it is a miracle that Joe wasn't hurt. I agree, God. I know that maybe the flying little angels that I dream about saved my family today. I still have nightmares about that rattlesnake hurting Paul and Joe. Sometimes I feel childish looking around the bed to see if a rattlesnake is hiding there. Please help me forget this terrible nightmare. Paul tries to pretend that everything is OK, but I think that he was shaken too. But enough about my story about the rattlesnake. I am sure you have seen worse.

Here is another one of my writings for you and your heavens.
Mirror, mirror, on the wall,
Today I will see...beautiful, colorful life unfolding,
in every dimension, in all directions.
In my focus...and out of my focus...and oh!
I see the life source in my reflection...
Here I go...let's dive into the day...
Good morning...sunshine...

Love and Respect, Always,
Sara

"Wow, I'm not sure how relaxed I am going to be working around here thinking about the rattlesnake's family living around here," Edward anxiously remarked.

"Don't worry, son. This place seems like poor breeding grounds. My wife and I never had children, and neither did Sara and Paul. So the poor snake probably didn't father any children either." The men couldn't help but laugh. Max continued, "I like her writings. She is very positive and interesting." Edward nodded.

CHAPTER FIVE

During the night after the rattlesnake reading, Edward wondered if the little angels in Sara's dreams had anything in common with the little angels in his. Since he couldn't make sense of any of it, he decided not to make much of the story, though he did check around his bed a few times to make sure there were no rattlesnakes there. Finally he was able to sleep.

The next morning after a breakfast of bread and cheese and strong black coffee, they went right into reading Sara's next letter.

Dear God,

I know that I always liked the color red, especially on your beautiful roses. But that was until I saw that rattlesnake's blood when Paul buried him. Now I cannot stand the color. Paul asked me to stay inside and not come out to look at the snake, but I couldn't help myself. Paul later thanked me for keeping Joe. They are very close these days. Perhaps Joe is one of your angels disguised as a dog.

So now maybe I can talk Paul into bringing in a child or two from the orphanage to live with us. God, give me the strength to convince him that we will be happier taking care of a child that doesn't have anyone in this world. I know that I could be a very good mother. I will start to pray again, and you can have some good words for me too. I am sure that Paul could be a great father too. Even though he doesn't want me to see his emotions, I find him to be a very sensitive man. He cares so much about how I feel about things. He doesn't act tough like other men. When I go to town, I hear from some wives that they are truly afraid of their husbands. I thank you for putting Paul in my life.

However, I still long for children. I don't understand why some people like us cannot have any. I have seen people with children that don't treat them right. Some people have more children than they can feed. I know that I'm not supposed to doubt you, but I have to be honest with you. I don't like it and I cannot accept it. One way or another you need to help me out here. I refuse to give up. I am writing down these requests. I feel surer of myself if I write things down. It helps clarify my needs. I expect a miracle. Only you can help me now. I will keep you posted.

Here is another one of my writings.
I rise today, like any other day, with the hidden rays
of smiles in the core of my heart...

"Good morning, God," the silent observer inside
whispers,
I hear the joy...I smile...
So much to love, so much to find, so much to see,
so much to feel...
I open a window to greet the day...as I breathe the
cool air,
It whispers, "Good morning," to my face.
Oh, the rays of joy, oh, the rays of God, slide down
my breath,
down to my heart, tickling my body with the beautiful,
joyous, smiling,
red little pieces of life,
As I observe as the observer, as me, as all in one.

With Love and Respect,
Sara

Edward was the first to speak. "Funny, the color red doesn't really appeal to me either. I guess I understand what Sara means. I hope that she convinced her husband to adopt a child, don't you?"

"We'll have to wait and see, I guess. Maybe if it wasn't for the rattlesnake, Paul wouldn't love Joe. So maybe another drama could convince him to adopt a child." Edward knew that Max had a good point. He placed the letters neatly on top of the coffee table and went outside to work on the porch.

As Edward was busy hammering nails into a new section of the porch, he noticed an old pickup truck approaching the driveway. He stopped and watched as it parked next to his own car. A plain woman got out from the driver's door and walked toward the porch. As she got closer, he could see her better. She looked to be in her thirties, with short, straight hair. She wore a blue long-sleeved shirt and jeans that looked too big for her.

"Hi there, you must be Ed." She spoke between and over the hammering.

Edward stood up and waited until she got closer. "Hello, how can I help you? Are you a friend of the owner?"

"Yes, I am. Is Max inside?" She didn't wait for Edward to respond. As she approached the door and walked inside, she looked at Edward and said that he could call her Kate.

Edward continued with his work. He could hear them inside laughing and talking very loudly. Max came out and asked Edward to join them. Even though Edward didn't care much to join them, he thought it would be polite to do so. No one could be pretty compared to his Lily, but why couldn't this Kate lady be a little pretty at least? He tried to stop himself from thinking those kinds of thoughts.

As it turned out, Kate was the neighbor who'd sent the sandwiches along with the fruits and vegetables. At Max's invitation, she was more than happy to come and read Sara's Dear God letters with the men. She caught up by reading the first three letters to herself and now eagerly waited for Edward to start the next one. Edward suggested that Kate should read the letters out loud, being the newcomer and a woman, like the author of the letters. But Max insisted that Sara surely would want their discoverer to read them.

Edward started reading.

Dear God,

I am so thankful. But because of the twin girls you had Paul bring home, I had no time to write. They are so adorable. Sometimes I think they actually look like Paul and me. The orphanage didn't know exactly how old they are, but even though they are very tall, I am sure they are six. For it was six years ago Christmas that I first prayed to you that Paul would agree to bring home a child from the orphanage. They are very quiet and don't want to play, but I am sure I can change all that. I so want to know what their names are, but Paul says the woman who worked at the orphanage didn't know either. I told them that I will call them Jane and Helen unless they tell me otherwise. I am going to celebrate their birthdays on Christmas so I can remember what miracles you gave me. As I look at my girls, my heart skips a beat. I already love them so much. God, I thank you for this blessing. You have given me more than I asked for. I have seen your miracles. I know Paul is deeply happy. How wonderful that he brought home two children for us to love. I have so much love to give that I don't know how to behave. Paul mostly spends his free time with Joe, but I am now a mother and too busy to worry about the two of them. I am sure they can manage. I have to go now to attend my children.

> Here is my gift to the heavens.
> With your lovely hands,
> Plant a deep red rose as beautiful as kindness,
> In an empty, lifeless, forgotten place.
> Maybe then the sky will fall in love,
> In love with the most precious rose.
> Maybe then it will rain from the lovesick heart of
> the sky.
> Maybe then the empty, lifeless, forgotten place will
> drink lots of rain,

And become alive, full of colors, full of flowers, full of
magical fragrances,
All because of your kind, lovely hands.

With Love and Respect,
Sara

Max, Kate, and Edward were smiling. It was wonderful to learn that Paul had finally adopted two girls from the orphanage. "Do you guys really believe that this is a true story?" Kate asked. "Could Sara have made up these letters to God just to while away her time?"

Edward couldn't believe his ears. "You shouldn't talk this way about these letters. No one asked us to sit here and read them. I personally see no reason why anyone would make up such a story. These are clearly letters written by this Sara lady to her God. I'm not sure about the reality of that God, but I know in my heart that they are real letters telling the real story."

Edward didn't know why he sensed a strong connection with Sara. He felt that he could have trusted her back then and that he trusted her now. He also felt that he had to protect her. He stood up, placed the stack of letters on the coffee table, then went outside and continued working on the porch. He was happy that Sara's prayers were answered even though he wasn't sure that the answer came from God or just pure luck.

Shortly after Edward resumed his work, Kate left the house. As she walked toward her truck, she stopped and apologized for questioning Sara's veracity, telling Edward that she agreed with him that Sara had really experienced everything that she wrote, adding that she hoped Edward wouldn't mind if she came back and listened to him reading the rest of the letters.

"Why do you have to ask me if you can come and listen? I'm sure Max will be happy to have you," Edward replied.

"I know, but you're the chosen one. We've been here all these years and the letters never revealed themselves. Now that you're here, they have. You're the one who was meant to find them. That's exactly why you're the one who must read them to us. I'm not sure what your religious background is, but there is something here you cannot ignore. Something beyond our comprehension is at work here."

"Of course you can come. I'm sorry if I gave you the idea that you aren't welcome. I think chance brought me here, but since it'll make it more exciting to believe that I'm the chosen one, I'm going to go along with you guys." Edward smiled. "How did you wind up in Little Falls?" he asked.

"This isn't a bad place if you get used to it. I came here a few years ago to relax and get away from a lot of things. Now I'm here. I really liked Sara's poem at the end of this last letter. Do you believe that one person can make such a difference, as she's suggesting?" Kate asked.

"Why not? I'm sure anything is possible," Edward answered.

Kate turned toward her pickup. "Gotta go, see you tomorrow." She would continue to mull over the letters and the fact that Edward was the one chosen to find them. Did God really choose him? Why him? Or was this just an accident? Maybe anyone else could have found the letters. But if this was God's handiwork, why did he wait so long before he revealed the letters?

Edward himself couldn't truly believe what had happened. He was stunned that Sara had asked God for children and that after much resistance her husband ended up adopting two daughters for them. If this wasn't a miracle, at least it was close to one.

Max came outside to see how things were going. Edward looked at him. "Boss, don't you think after finishing the porch we should open up and redo this house piece by piece? We might find a hidden treasure or something. What if this Sara lady also hid some of her fine jewelry? Think about it. They would be old and pricey by now."

Max smiled. "Son, it's wiser to keep reading her letters first. If she hid some treasure, don't you think she would tell God exactly where she hid it? It doesn't look like she's hiding anything from God." The men laughed.

The next day Edward, Max, and Kate sat while Edward read Sara's next letter.

Dear God,

As you surely understand, I am writing to you only when something happens that is out of the ordinary. For I have to be discrete and write only when no one sees me. And now that my girls are a little older, it takes me a long time to home school them. So I'm sorry I haven't written sooner.

Thank you for helping Jane and Helen open up to me. As you know, I cried the first day they started to talk. They have voices of angels.

Today Paul brought home a letter from my parents. My mother is sick now and she wishes to see me. I am very worried about her, God. I talked with Paul and he is going to arrange that I go with the girls to see her for a few weeks. Please help her through this. I'm also worried about Paul. He doesn't eat much. I'm glad that Joe will be here with him while I'm gone. Please take care of everything. I'll miss him very much. I didn't think it was going to be so hard for me to leave him for a short time. As is his way, he's not saying much, but I know that he's going to miss me too. I can see it in his eyes. I'll write after my trip. Wish me luck.

Here is my writing for your heavens.
With hope I live inside the unknown.
I hope for the best, while life shows me some sorrow.
I cry the sorrows of life and laugh the joys of my days.
I watch everything change, and change as everything
passes.
I love and live, I do and I am, I change with everything.
Everything changes.

Love and Respect,
Sara

Edward, Max, and Kate looked at one another and silently agreed that this letter was short enough that they would go through one more without any breaks.

Edward continued.

Dear God,

I know I haven't written for over a year now. I didn't have the courage to; I was so upset with you. I just couldn't understand why my mother had to die before I arrived. I had so much that I wanted to tell her. And Jane and Helen wanted to meet their grandmother. So much has changed. I'm grateful at least that you let me be there later for my father. It helped him to see his granddaughters. It was so worthwhile that I ended up staying there longer than I expected. I got none of such time with my mother. Please, God, tell her for me that I love her very much. Tell her that I don't hate her for persuading me to marry Paul. I do love him. Please ask her to come to my dreams sometimes. Please tell her that I am living a happy life. I have everything that I ever wanted. I just miss her very much.

Now that I have written what I had to tell you about my mother, I hope you have forgiven me for being angry with you for the past year. I now want to thank you for giving Jane back to us. I almost thought that, since her fevers weren't going down, we were going to lose her. I couldn't help my little angel. I'm not sure if you answered my prayers or Pauls and Helen's. It really doesn't matter to me. Jane is better now and that is all that counts. Today Paul didn't go to work so he could spend some time with us. Looking at Paul and Jane and Helen and Joe playing together meant so much to me. God, I thank you for all of my blessings.

Here it goes for the heavens.
We are all in the same boat.
We are all from the same source.
From the unknown we have arrived.
Into the unknown we will go back.
Please, little angels, tell me some secrets.
Share with me your most inner sights.
My eyes aren't made to see too far.
Be my light, be my sight.

With Love and Respect,
Sara

CHAPTER SIX

Edward thought of all the things he would have told his parents. If he had been just as confident as Sara was, he could have actually talked to them. That night he asked God to please ask his parents to come to his dreams. In his thoughts he told his mother about all his pain and hurt. He told her how Lily had left him before he took the opportunity to tell her about his big dreams, because he was too afraid that she would find them silly and childish. He told his mother how reading Sara's writings inspired his own dream of becoming a writer. He knew what a good story felt like, but he had forgotten what he always knew. He wanted to have faith like Sara did. How this woman could write to God so easily, as if she was talking to an old friend, mystified him. He admired her total faith. It was as if she had no doubts. He wished that he could have just a little of her faith.

Edward cried himself to sleep that night. He cried the way he had when he was a boy in his mother's arms—on the day he had to leave for school for the very first time, without his mother at his side. Edward didn't dream about his parents. He dreamt about five or six little angels flying around him where he was sleeping, and he felt very blessed.

Kate arrived early the next day with a big bag of groceries. She had decided to cook breakfast for everyone. Edward was almost done with the porch, but he wasn't ready to leave this part of his life. He definitely wanted to finish Sara's letters, especially since Max had made it clear that he wanted Edward to be the one who read the letters. Max had left earlier for his morning walk, so Edward went inside to see if Sara needed help in the kitchen, though she didn't look like a woman who needed any. He gratefully heard her say she could use his company.

"You never told me why you chose a place like this to live," Edward said.

"I don't live here, Ed, I am here temporarily. I said that I came here to get away from a lot of stuff, but I didn't say what I was leaving behind. When I came here a few years ago, Max literally saved my life. I simply didn't want to live anymore."

Edward felt bad for asking Kate to talk. He assured her that she didn't have to tell him anything, that they could talk about the letters.

"It's OK, Ed. It will help me share my story. If God chose you to read Sara's Dear God letters, then I can tell you my story. Well, if you could've seen me then, you wouldn't have recognized me. I had very long hair. I wouldn't have been caught dead in casual clothes. My nails were always done, and I was so proud of how I carried myself. I was on top of the world those days. I lived in New York City and worked for a large law firm. I was clerking part-time to make a little money while I was going to school to become a paralegal. I trusted the three attorneys that were running the firm. I had no reason not to. One late afternoon, as I had just arrived to my apartment, my cell phone rang. The woman's voice on the other end was unfamiliar to me. She was crying and asked me to meet with her right away. She was the wife of one of the partners in the firm and found my number on her husband's cell phone. She would explain everything to me once we met in person, since she couldn't trust talking on her cell phone. I agreed to meet with her in a coffee shop within walking distance to where I lived.

"I arrived on time to find her already there. After making me swear that I wouldn't tell anyone about our conversation, she explained that she trusted me because her husband had always talked about the kind and honest person that I was. Pale white and trembling, she began her story. She was afraid for her life, suspecting that her husband wanted her dead. Shocked and frightened, I asked her why she wasn't going to the police instead. She asked that I not interrupt her so she could tell me everything. Evidence for her fear was on one of his two cell phones. She didn't find it on his personal one, so she concluded it must be on the one in his office. She asked me to open the office for her, since I had access to the alarm code and keys, and she didn't.

"I didn't know what to do. She was certain that going through the legal system would be impossible. I don't know why, but I knew in my heart that she was telling the truth. I explained that using the code for the after-hours building entrance would make me legally liable should something go missing. I wasn't sure that I was willing to put my life on the line. She pleaded that she just wanted to take pictures of the incoming and outgoing phone numbers so that nothing would go missing. She knew exactly where her husband kept the cell phone. Once when she dropped something off for him, she saw him place the phone behind a certain law book. Initially alarmed at the risk she was asking me to take, I calmed myself by estimating that the whole task would probably take us less than five minutes, reminding myself that, after all, it wasn't unusual for me to return to the office after hours to get my purse or some other personal item that I had forgotten to take with me.

"Once I decided, I drove immediately to the office. She was to meet me there in ten minutes and was already there when I arrived. Thinking of nothing but the task ahead, I unlocked the building door, ushered her in before me, and walked with her toward the building elevator. While going up, we looked at each other like two strangers who had just happened to get on together. As soon as the elevator door opened, I walked toward our office door and unlocked it. I waved to her to go inside while I decoded the alarm. She went right to her husband's office door, which luckily was unlocked. I was terrified, suddenly realizing that I would be too afraid to work there anymore.

"Three minutes later, on schedule, she quickly walked out of the office and we headed out. I put the alarm back on and locked the office door. We hurried back to the elevator and all but ran to the front lobby. By then it was quite dark outside. We managed to open the door and stood there for a second to say our good-byes.

Then it happened. Something hard came down on the back of her head. She had no time to scream. I screamed so loud that I shocked her assailant, who hadn't seen me with her. The police told me later that he must have been following her earlier, seen her going toward the building, but missed us entering together. He turned around and ran as fast as he could. All I could do was scream for help and dial 911.

"I tried to control her bleeding and kept shouting at her to stay with me. I went to the hospital with her since she pleaded for me not to leave her alone. I couldn't shake the feeling that I was somehow to blame, since she wouldn't have been there if I hadn't helped her.

"There were a lot of police interviews and a lot of sleepless nights. Everyone at work found out what had happened. I never returned there to work, unable to face any of them again. Since I never saw the assailant, I was never called as a witness, which spared me from having to follow the case to the bitter end. I did hear that the poor woman lived through her nightmare. I also found out that her husband went on trial for attempted murder, but don't know whether he was convicted. I had to leave New York City. I couldn't walk through the streets without remembering that horrific scene. One of the police detectives told me that if it wasn't for me being there that guy would have probably finished her." With a long sigh of relief, Kate concluded, "At least now I can talk about it."

By now Kate had finished making breakfast. Edward had new respect for this woman. She had risked her job to help a desperate stranger and in doing so saved that woman's life. "Do you think you'll ever be ready to leave this place?" Edward asked.

"Not before we're finished reading Sara's letters," Kate laughed.

"How did you come to know Max?" Edward asked.

"I knew him before all that. He was like an uncle to me as I was growing up as an Army brat in the same camp where he served. When he heard what had happened, he asked me to come here. I'm staying in one of Max's other places. I look after the fruits and veg- etables and share them with Max, and I occasionally cook for him. The location and the regimen have given me the peace I need."

Edward didn't say a word. The two of them seemed perfectly content to eat in silence. They drank their coffee and finished eat- ing the vegetable omelets that Kate had prepared.

Max opened the door with his usual smile and walked in to join in the great omelet. "You kids getting ready to read another letter?" As Kate helped fill Max's plate, Edward began reading Sara's next letter.

Dear God,

It has been a long time—too long—since I have written to you. I haven't wanted to write to you about this situation. I thought I could handle it by myself. But I guess I need your help. At least I am brave enough to admit it. I know that I am supposed to love my neighbor. At least this is what most of us here on earth believe. But do we have to love a neighbor that isn't kind? I am sure you know who I am talking about. This Mrs. Howard isn't a nice person. Even though I am trying my best to make myself be kind to her, I'm not sure how to continue. Paul says that I am being very childish and that Mrs. Howard is only trying to be my friend. She always comes over unannounced and she makes the girls feel very uncomfortable. (She criticizes everything I do. Even when she gives me a rare compliment, it is part of a criticism. The other day, she began by telling me that I am too good for Paul, then faulted me for attending to him so much.) I asked her to stop. Last week, she brought me and the girls some kind of chicken stew. In spite of its horrible taste, we all ate some to be polite and were sick the whole next day. Helen says that she probably prays some witchcraft on the food, but Helen is just angry and doesn't mean anything. Anyway, I am sorry that I told Paul that I thought Mrs. Howard was trying to poison us. Paul didn't like what I said. Sometimes when I think of Mrs. Howard, I think that she must have a good heart. I see that she married a man more than twice her age. He gets sick a lot and she is always taking care of him. Lately it seems like he has been getting too many food poisonings, so maybe she should quit cooking for him. Sorry, God, I know that I shouldn't judge people. But I cannot help but think with all the money her husband has, why don't they make sure that his food is freshly prepared? Now I know that I am talking about things that aren't my business. Please forgive me; I just wanted to tell you everything. I think you already know what I am thinking, so there should be no harm for me to admit to you what you already know.

Please continue to look after my girls. They are getting older now and are always running around the town and playing around the lake, so watch them for me.

Here is a piece I wrote for the heavens.
What is left from a life, when it is gone?
What is left behind, from all this up and down?
What is left after we are no longer feeling?
What is left to be remembered when the memory fades?
What is left to be touched, after touch is no longer?
What is left to be affected, when the time is up?
Only my love will remain behind me after I am gone.
Nothing else matters, then and now, so love with love, and love.

Love and Respect,
Sara

As Edward finished reading, he looked up and saw that Kate and Max were waiting for him to continue. "Are you sure you want me to continue?"

"Yes," replied Kate. "If it is OK with Max, I want to hear one more."

"Don't stop on my account. The main reason that I insist on waiting in between these letters is that we give respect and more attention to them. We will have more time to think about them. But one more letter can't hurt anyone. Go for it," Max replied.

Edward continued.

Dear God,

I am so worried now. Why do you choose different religions for people? We are all the same. We can love each other the same. When Helen asked me why, when she was younger, men and boys used to wear dark, round hats on their heads all the time and now no one does, I was shocked. In the past, when they told me that they had never seen a Christmas tree, I assumed that they must have been poor. She told me that the men sometimes had very long beards. I don't know how to handle this, God. I haven't said anything to Paul. Please forgive me for hiding this from him. I can't lose my daughters. I know Paul loves them as his own children. But what happens when he finds out that they were born in a Jewish family? How could this have happened in the orphanage? What would Paul do? Could he become angry? I know that he developed a strong bond with them in the past six years, but I am afraid. What would the community say? I told Helen that she must have dreamt that boys and men were wearing special round hats, and that I must have told her and Jane a lot of bedtime stories that made her think that way. I told her that she isn't supposed to share her thoughts with anyone except me. I hope she listens.

God, please help me come to peace with this situation. You know that I don't care what family or religious backgrounds my girls came from. I just want everything to be OK. I have complete faith in you to make everything OK. I think it will be simpler if no one ever found out about Helen and Jane's background. What is the difference anyways? I don't see any difference. We are all the same. Sometimes people just make things more complicated when they learn some information. We are all human beings. We are all sharing this world. You can hear us from different parts of the world, with whatever religion we have. I don't think you care what we look like or what our background is or what religion we use to contact you. Anyways, I know that you love us the same. That is exactly why I have faith that you will make sure that everything is going to be all right.

Please forgive me for keeping this from Paul.
Here is something I wrote for your heavens.
I cannot see the differences. My, I must be blind.
I cannot hear our separateness in our voices. I must be deaf.
I cannot feel how one life isn't worth as much as another.
I cannot see how colors cannot blend together or shine one by one.
To me, all is one and the same. What's life is life, what's worthy is worthy.
To me, the parts of all are one. To me, all life is worthy.

With Love and Respect,
Sara

CHAPTER SEVEN

Edward put the letter down with a puzzled look. "Why would this poor woman have to bear all of this now? After believing that her dream of having children had come true, why would God give her more to worry about?"

"It must have been a very scary situation for Sara," Max replied. "I think, those days, there was no mixing of religions. I'm not sure if adopting from a different religion was even allowed."

Kate asked the men if they were ready for fresh coffee. As she was making a new pot, she told them that she thought that it was wonderful that Helen and Jane came from a Jewish family and were adopted by a Christian family.

Kate had to leave after coffee. Edward and Max decided to go for a walk. "OK, Ed, since we're thinking about God and all, I'm going to take you to a very special place."

Edward smiled to himself and said, "I hope you're not going to get religious on me or take me to a church or something."

"Don't worry about that, son. This place isn't man-made at all. When we get there, you'll find out why it's so special. It's not too far from here, about an hour away."

The men walked in silence. Edward thought about his life and his plans. He knew that soon he'd be putting the finishing touches on the porch. He also knew that Sara's letters had greatly affected him already. He admired Sara for her courage. He was secretly glad that he didn't have to experience being a woman and that he didn't have to live in the time that Sara lived. He worried about her. Even though it sounded foolish, he was hoping that God had actually listened to her and had helped her with her requests. He couldn't understand why people separated themselves from each other because of their unique religious background. Why couldn't everyone be free to co-exist and love whoever they wanted without any restrictions? If Sara were alive now, after so many years, she would see the world still experiencing a lot of prejudices. What would she say to God if she could write another letter today?

They were halfway to their destination. "Isn't it sad that women had to go through such hard times back then?" Edward asked.

"Yes it is," Max replied. "They're still going through a lot of hardships. The problems have changed, but the challenges are still real and difficult. You see, Ed, the female species in all creations is the weaker species. It is always harder to face life challenges when you don't have the upper hand."

"I think that is why woman are created a little smarter, to compensate for their weaker physique," Edward said.

"If my wife was alive today, I'm sure she'd have some kind of a clever answer for you, but at this moment I just can't come up one," Max replied.

They crossed a small creek to find many colorful plants that were unknown to Edward. He was amazed at how beautiful the natural surroundings were. No wonder Max walked every morning to experience the peace and beauty here. Edward strolled with great inner comfort, knowing that he was meant to walk this path, that this moment in time was meant to be for him.

Suddenly Max stopped and signaled with his hand for Edward to stop, then motioned for him to follow very quietly and slowly. After a few minutes they arrived. They stood in front of one of the biggest and most beautiful trees that Edward had ever seen. The trunk was awesome in height, breadth, and form. Edward couldn't even guess its height, which disappeared into the sky. The roots were partially outside the soil covering a large part of the surrounding ground. The effect was of a kneeling woman, skirt spread about her, with the blue-green leaves like feathered arms moving back and forth in slow motion with the wind. Max said hello to the tree. Edward couldn't help but say hello as well.

"How in God's name is this possible?" Edward asked.

"Don't talk about her as if she cannot hear you. Are you sure that there are only two of us here?" Max asked.

Edward knew what Max was talking about, but he had to adjust himself to this new idea. "I'm happy to meet you. My name is Edward. I'm sure you know my friend here," Edward said, looking at the tree. Both men knelt in front of the tree, trying to adopt her posture.

"Edward, I've known her for a long time now. I wish I knew her story. I sit here like this every day hoping to hear her story," Max said.

"Maybe it's her who hears your story," Edward replied.

Max smiled. "I call her Lady. Don't you think Lady suits her?"

Impishly, Edward replied, "Yes. Does she call you Max or Sir Major?" They laughed at their private joke. After their initial contemplation of Lady, Edward rose and walked around her. He protectively avoided stepping on her roots as he approached to touch her trunk. The men decided to nap next to it.

Edward began dreaming about the small flying angels, now flying around Lady's branches. He saw the blue sky peeking through the branches, which were calmly moving back and forth with the wind, beckoning his breath to follow. The wind blowing among the branches was the same wind that was filling his lungs with air. As he relaxed further into the dream, his breath became the tree and the tree his breath. Two of the small angels came down where Edward was sleeping and sat weightlessly on his knees. As he watched them converse, he tried to hear what they were saying, but they spoke too softly.

The angel on Edward's left knee turned his little face smilingly toward him. "Hello, Edward Evans."

Astoundingly, Edward could hear the angel's voice inside his chest. "Hi there, little angel. I've seen you before in my dreams, but I don't know your name." Edward was even more astounded to hear his own voice inside his chest even though his lips weren't moving.

"I am here," the angel replied. The angel sitting on Edward's right knee had jumped up and resumed playing with the other angels. But the one conversing with Edward sat patiently and looked straight at him.

"I know you are here, little one. Who are you?" Edward continued to hear his own voice resound loudly inside his chest.

The little angel replied, "I am always here. You keep going back and forth in your thoughts, but now you are here. I could never get your attention before."

Edward was confused. He wasn't getting the clarity that he wanted from this little guy, but he wasn't going to let go of this opportunity of a lifetime. He had so many questions that he wanted to ask, but he didn't know where to begin. Looking straight at the angel, he blurted out, "Do you come here often?"

"I am always here," the little angel replied.

"I mean, here beside Lady? I mean, beside this tree?" Edward asked.

The little angel explained, "I am here with you and your friend and the tree and the sky and the soil and the wind. I am here now."

Edward smiled and thanked the little angel. He didn't feel like asking him any other questions. He just wanted to watch him. The little angel jumped up on one of the tree's branches and joined the others. They had faces of little cute children and were just as playful, but Edward figured that they must be angels because they had wings. From the perfect view from where he was lying, he watched them play on the tree. He kept hearing a tone of music that he couldn't recognize. As the music started to play, the little angels would stop giggling and would just stay still, and as soon as the music stopped, they would start jumping up and down. They were playing some kind of a game with the music, which Edward was hearing from inside his chest. He tried to pay close attention to it, which had a kind of melody that he had never heard before. It also had a timbre that was something between violin and guitar. Curious, he called up to the little angel to ask what it was that he was hearing.

Without any hesitation, the angel flew down close to Edward's left ear and replied, "The music is Lady's voice." He then quickly jumped back up on the tree and continued his giggles with the rest of his angel friends.

"Son, are you ready to leave? Edward? Son, are you ready to leave yet?" Max was looking down at Edward, whispering in his right ear to wake him up gently. The men turned around to return home. After a few steps, Edward turned back to the tree. "Goodbye, Lady. Thank you for your hospitality." Max smiled, looked at the tree, and gave her a quick little bow.

The next day Edward completed the porch, satisfied with the job he had done. He remembered the days of helping his father and how satisfying it felt to look at a perfectly done job. Smiling proudly, he walked into the house. Max was sitting on the couch, reading a book. He looked up at Edward. "Well done, Ed. You deserve a drink. And I have the perfect red wine to start our celebration." Edward smiled and sat down on the other side of the couch, the first time he had ever done so. Usually he sat on one of the chairs by the kitchen table.

Max continued, "Edward, I haven't forgotten about your pay. Are you ready to talk about it now?"

Edward paused and then said, "Not really. I don't really think that I'm done yet."

Max smiled. "I know that you're not done here. We still have to finish Sara's letters. I just wanted to mention the pay so you know that I appreciate everything you've done. The porch looks better than I expected."

They sat there and talked about the porch and the details of the job for another half hour. Then they heard Kate's footsteps coming toward the house. She knocked on the door and called out, "Hello, are you guys in?" She opened the door and walked in.

CHAPTER EIGHT

Edward couldn't believe his eyes. Kate looked very different. She was wearing a blue dress along with a white sun hat and slippers. Her face was glowing and she seemed unusually happy. Edward had never seen her this way before. She looked beautiful. He was glad that he knew her, suddenly realizing that he always felt better when he saw her. Though he couldn't put his finger on it, there was something about her that made him feel good about himself.

Max stood up and greeted her. "Kate dear, you look like the girl that I remember. Where were you all this time? Welcome back to your life."

Kate laughed and said, "Thank you, Max. I am extraordinarily happy and content today. I was able to sleep like a baby last night. I had absolutely no worries. It's so gorgeous outside, I say we sit on this beautiful new porch and read another of Sara's letters."

Edward stood up to grab the letters from the coffee table. "I'm going to vote yes on reading outside," he responded warmly. Smiling, Max followed them outside, grabbing the wine bottle and glasses on the way to enhance the spirit of the reading.

Edward began reading Sara's next letter.

Dear God,

Thank you for all of my blessings. I am truly happy. Today Paul told me to start preparing for a big Thanksgiving. I love Thanksgiving, even though it gets colder. The air is clearer and invigorating, and nature looks calm and beautiful. My girls love the holidays too, as they get to thinking about their Christmas presents. This year I am going to make sure they get very special ones. This year Paul is unusually happy about the holidays. He is going to bring home a big juicy turkey for me to cook. I am so very lucky. Jane and Helen are getting new clothes and are going to pick out a dress for me too. I hope the next few weeks last a long time. Paul wants to invite a few of his coworkers to our home for Thanksgiving dinner. I am going to have Jessie come with her family too. She is a wonderful friend, my best friend, for whom I am very thankful. Please make this Thanksgiving dinner perfect and memorable for us. I will write you afterwards.

Here is something from me for the heavens.
Let's celebrate with joy and giving, let's drink to the heavens, my darling.
Let's bake the sweetest pies in loving, let's share the scents of fall in color.
Let's greet the season's warmth in cooking.

With Love and Respect,
Sara

Getting up, Edward announced, "Reading about all of that good food makes me hungry. What do you guys say if we head to town for some nice pie?" Everyone agreed. Max went upstairs to get his hat.

Edward looked forward to spending time with Kate. She was easy to talk to. He told her that he was a sad that the porch was already finished. As they were talking, they heard a loud noise from inside the house. They ran toward the sound, calling for Max. He had slipped and fallen down the stairs. Kate ran toward him and grabbed his shoulders. He was sitting on the floor, a little disoriented. "Are you OK, Max? What happened? How did you fall?" she asked anxiously.

Edward stood watching the two of them. He asked if he should call for help. Max looked up and replied, "No need to call anyone. I got dizzy and couldn't control myself, then slipped and fell down. I do feel a very sharp pain in my right ankle."

Kate looked at Edward. "I think we have to take him to a doctor. There's a hospital not too far from here. Help me take him to the car, please."

Max didn't argue. Edward and Kate managed to hold him by the shoulders and help him to Edward's car. After they eased him into the front passenger seat, Kate got in the back. As Edward drove, Max and Kate gave him directions. Kate kept her left hand on Max's shoulder as they were driving.

At the hospital, the nurse took Max in right away. Everyone at the hospital knew him and gave him special attention. Edward could see how the nurses and the rest of the staff were on a first-name basis with him. Edward assumed they were responding to Max's ability to make people around him very comfortable. He was down-to-earth, with a cool and collected attitude that contributed to making him an exceptional listener, better than anyone Edward had ever met.

Edward and Kate sat in the waiting area looking worried. She told him she was concerned about Max's dizziness. She hoped it didn't mean anything serious. She placed her face in her palms and started to cry. Trying to make her feel better, Edward assured her that Max would be OK. "Look at how strong and healthy he looks. I am sure he's going to be just fine. Maybe he was just tired and dehydrated. Let's not jump to any conclusions." He got up, picked up a few napkins from the table in the corner of the waiting room, and handed them to Kate. He placed his hand on her shoulder to help her calm down.

She looked up and thanked him. "You're right," she said, "He's going to be fine. I feel a little dependent on Max. I'm not sure if that's a good thing or not. He's like family to me. My own parents never had time for me. They were very busy traveling and vacationing and were into their friends and their own routines. I don't blame them for that, but Max has always been there for me like a father. Sometimes I want to stay in this town to make sure Max will be OK."

Edward understood what Kate was talking about. He wished he had someone like Max to talk to also. Max was a very special person. He understood why everyone in Little Falls knew Max and respected him. "I'm happy that I met him too. I wouldn't have if I hadn't been laid off and my fiancée hadn't left me. I was engaged and Lily, my ex, broke it off as soon as she found out that I didn't have a paying job. I can't believe how stupid I was. How didn't I see that she didn't really love me?"

Kate paused and said, "You shouldn't blame yourself now. The important thing is that you're clear with yourself. You've learned a great lesson. I bet that somewhere inside of you there was a tiny lingering voice telling you that Lily didn't love you the way you deserved it. Or even that you were in a wrong place. Or maybe she was there to teach you that you should value yourself more than you did. Keep the lesson, but let go of regrets. Life is full of lessons. Sometimes they're unfair. I guess that's how we grow."

Sitting in the waiting area, they turned to some local news on the television. A few hours had passed when a nurse walked toward them with a smile. "The good news is that all of Max's tests are fine, but the bad news is that he broke his foot in three places. The doctor wants to keep him here tonight for observation. You folks can leave tonight and come back in the morning to pick him up."

On the way back, Edward told Kate that he could drop her off at her place first and pick her up the next day. He didn't think it was a good idea for her to drive by herself at night. Kate thanked him for his thoughtfulness. As they were driving together, Edward wished the ride would take longer, that all the traffic lights would turn red. Driving with Kate next to him gave him a warm feeling. He wondered if Kate felt the same way. As he pulled into her driveway, he parked and got out of the car. He wanted to open the door for her, but by the time he reached her side, Kate had already gotten out. As they walked toward her doorway, Edward stopped and let Kate continue into the house.

She paused at the door, turned to thank him, and asked, "What time will you pick me up tomorrow?"

"I'll pick you up around nine." He turned around and walked to his car.

On his way to Max's house, Edward thought about the events of that day: how he cared for Max and how thankful he was that Max was OK. He also recalled how Sara always made sure to thank God in her letters for every blessing she had. He thanked God in his heart for the two new friends that he had met in a time when he needed them the most. He thought about how Kate had looked that night, so different from how he had seen her the first time they met. She looked very good to him. He wanted to remember forever how she looked. His circle for that day was complete. When he arrived at the house, he was so tired that he went right to sleep.

The next morning Edward woke up around seven. He took a quick shower and made some fresh coffee. It felt incomplete not to have Max and Kate there to share the coffee with him. He decided to make some breakfast for himself. What would Max cook if he were here? He opened the refrigerator, took out a couple of eggs, and scrambled them. He was playing around with his cell phone and eating his breakfast when his phone rang. It was Lily!

CHAPTER NINE

When Edward saw Lily's phone number on his caller ID, he was shocked and angry. What was she going to want from him now? He feared she might disturb the peace he had found here in Little Falls. He was curious to know what she wanted from him, but he wasn't ready to talk with her. So he let the phone ring until the call went to his voice mail. He waited impatiently until a short ring alerted him that she had left a message. As he dialed his voice mail he imagined several scenarios of what she would say. He finally heard a low, weak voice, "Edward... honey, we need to talk. Call me as soon as you get this message. I am doing better now. I am ready to talk to you. Please call me. Can't wait to hear your voice. Miss you."

Edward was angry. Who did she think she was? He didn't need to talk to her. She didn't care about him. He had grown out of their relationship and had more peace without her than with her. But he still wanted to hear her voice. He didn't like feeling weak, but he kept thinking about the good times they had shared together. He remembered how he proposed to her and how happy she was to say yes to him. They drove to her parents' house right away to share their good news. He could still have that life. He could put everything back together.

He also remembered how she had looked at his mother's ring and talked about eventually changing it to a different one that would be suitable to show to her parents. Edward had been so appalled that he had failed to respond to Lily's comment. He had told himself that he simply had to accept her the way she was. He now realized that she needed to change him to accommodate her needs. Yes, she did wear his mother's ring, but she kept telling everyone that this was only the first ring, which was going to get upgraded soon. Edward had been hurt and angered by those comments. Now he was very confused. He wished she had never called. He thought that she probably needed something. Maybe she forgot something in his apartment. Maybe she had a fight with Lucy and needed Edward to hear her side of the story. Whatever it was, it made Edward angry.

He got up and washed the dishes while looking out the kitchen window. He didn't have to make any decisions now. He remembered that one of his college professors used to say in class, "If you're not sure what to do, just be ice. Do nothing and wait. It is better not to do anything if you're confused." He liked that suggestion. He was going to be ice about this situation now. He would talk this over with Max. He suddenly realized that he didn't want Kate to know about this call. He hoped that he and she wouldn't be in the car together if Lily called again. He went to the bathroom and looked at himself in the mirror. He started shaving his beard for the first time since he came to this house. He brushed his shoulder length hair back. He looked pretty good. He looked different from the Edward he used to know, but couldn't say exactly how. He did look bolder. He smiled at his image and walked out to his car.

Edward arrived in front of Kate's place at 8:45. He got out of the car and walked toward her house. He wondered what color she would be wearing. As he approached, thinking she might not be ready since he was a little early, she opened the door. "My, you look handsome, Edward," Kate greeted him, smiling as she opened the door in a peach-color top and nice-fitting jeans.

Edward was nervous and happy to hear her say that. "I decided it was time to shave. I like shaving once every month or so." He smiled. She stepped out, closing the door after her.

"I called the hospital and talked with Max this morning," Kate informed him.

"How is he doing?"

"He's doing great. He said he couldn't wait for us to pick him up and go home so he could listen to Sara's next letter." They both laughed.

This time Edward walked faster than Kate so he could open the car door for her. She smiled and got in. He was confused about how he felt. He had to be nice. He wasn't going to make any moves until he was sure. He couldn't hurt Kate. She was too nice and too important to him. The thought of asking Kate for a date kept popping into his mind. But he wasn't going to do that. He couldn't be sure about his feelings for Lily now that she had called. He tried to think of other things. He tried to think of Sara's letters. He was thinking what Sara might say to him if she knew him.

When they arrived at the hospital, the same nurse they spoke with the night before stood behind the counter. She greeted them warmly and asked them to follow her to the room where Max was waiting for them. He was sitting in a chair beside a bed, reading a newspaper. He looked up and said, "Hello, kids, how are you?"

"The more important question is how are you, Max?" Kate said.

Edward continued, "If you didn't want to pay for the pie, sir, you should have said so! Really, we would have been happy to pick up the bill!"

"Fine, fine, fine...and as for the sweet pie... that is a very good idea. I'm happy to go for it now. I'm just sad that I can't go for my morning walks for a while. Getting around is going to be a little tough for the next couple of weeks with this cast on my foot."

"Don't worry, boss, I'm sure you'll manage. You'll be walking soon. The nurse here was telling us that she was going to let us borrow a wheelchair for you. I'm not sure how you feel about someone else pushing you around, but it might be good for you. I know I don't mind pushing you around," Edward said with a smile.

Edward dropped Kate off at her house on the way to Max's. When they all gathered at Max's shortly afterwards, they realized that they still wanted that pie. Since it was too hard for Max to be traveling around, Kate volunteered to go to town and pick up a pie for everyone. That evening they sat around the kitchen table waiting for Edward to read another letter from Sara.

Dear God,

The Thanksgiving dinner was wonderful. Everything tasted great. There was plenty of food for everyone. Helen and Jane looked so grown up in their new pink and white dresses. Paul gave me a lot of compliments on my new green dress. I would have never picked green for myself if Helen hadn't insisted.

I wrote to you before about Mrs. Howard. I don't know what to say to Jessie about her. Paul says that I shouldn't say anything about her to anyone. I know he is right. I know that I'm not supposed to judge her. Jessie told me in confidence that she believes that Mrs. Howard is trying to poison her husband. I have been suspicious about it too. But every time I say something to Paul, he tells me that I am imagining things. Well, I know that Mr. Howard is a very old man, but he still could have a lot of years to live. I keep thinking about the poor man and how sad it is if our suspicions are true. I cannot do anything about these feelings. Maybe I should tell Jessie that I also share her feelings about them. I don't want to start any gossip. I am confused. I will pray so I know what to do. Please help me do the right thing.

> Here is a little something for the heavens.
> Light my way, pull me through, help me see the clues.
> Come with me, walk with me, hold my hand at night and darkness.
> Keep me safe, keep me focused, watch me pass the moments.
> Show me the way, show me the truth, help me see your clues.

Love and Respect,
Sara

As Edward finished the letter, he looked up to see if everyone agreed to stop reading for now and do something else. Kate was glad to stop. She said that she had some things that she had to take care of and that she could continue the next day. Max was fine with that. Edward stood at the door until Kate left the driveway. He was sad to see her go, but this would give him an opportunity to talk to Max about Lily's phone call.

Returning inside, Edward told Max about Lily's message. Max paused, then told Edward that this was a decision that only he could make. Edward confessed, "I'm a bit confused. I don't know what to do about this. It would have been so much easier if she had never called me back. But now she wants us to get back together. I could tell from her message."

"What do you want?" Max asked.

Edward thought about it for a minute and told Max that he didn't know what he wanted. "I'm angry at Lily. I can't believe she broke up our engagement without any hesitation over something that wasn't my fault. She didn't even give me a chance to explain myself."

Max looked at Edward. "And you are starting to develop feelings for Kate? That must be confusing you all the more."

Edward didn't know what to say. He hadn't realized that his inner thoughts and feelings for Kate were so obvious. He had tried to hide them. He felt so silly. What if Kate already knew how he felt? That would be terrible. He didn't want to confuse or hurt Kate. He didn't know what he wanted out of life. "I messed up, boss. You need to help me. Please tell me what to do and I'll do it."

Max smiled at his friend. "You know I can't tell you what to do. First of all, you wouldn't listen anyway. You'll wind up doing what you want to do in the long run, so you just have to see what feels right to you and do it. Who is the right woman for you? You'll live in regret if you let others make decisions for you. You see, son? Take your time if you need more time. There's no shortage of time now. There are moments in life that we have to make a choice. It looks like Lily already made a choice to leave you. You're not engaged to her anymore. She had already broken it off with you. You're a free man. Stop acting as if you're a prisoner. Do what you want to do. If you want to go back to Lily, that's your choice. You already know what you'll have with her. But please be a man about it. You can call Lily and not be so afraid of her. You two aren't in a relationship anymore. It doesn't matter what she says. You have your ring back. If you want to be with Lily, be with her. Do it with your whole heart. The man who does things half-heartedly will never be satisfied." Using an old cane that he had around the house, Max limped toward the kitchen. Edward excused himself to go for a walk. He needed to clear his head.

Edward started walking in the direction that Max had taken him when they first encountered Lady. He thought seeing her might help him. He had walked for just a few minutes when his cell phone rang. It was Lily's number. He picked up the phone.

"Hello," Edward answered.

"Good thing you picked up the phone. I was getting worried about you. Where are you? How come you haven't answered my call?" the voice in the phone demanded.

"How are you doing?" Edward asked.

"I am fine. Honey, when are you coming home?"

"Listen, Lily…please don't call me 'honey' anymore. It doesn't feel right. You need to respect my wishes if you want me to con- tinue with this conversation," Edward firmly asserted. He waited for Lily to respond, but she was obviously shocked and listening for him to continue. Edward complied, "I'm not coming back to you. I won't continue something that you already broke off. I have a lot of healing to do. But I do wish you well. So please let me be. We aren't together anymore. You need to close this chapter too. You are the one who wanted it over, so now it is over." Edward couldn't believe that he was the same man whom Lily could always boss around. He had changed. She didn't have her hook in him anymore, even though he was sometimes confused about that. It was no longer her business to know that, so he didn't mention it. He hoped that Lily wouldn't call anymore and he wouldn't have to face her again.

But Lily wasn't one to give up so easily. She accepted that they weren't engaged but wanted to meet with him and explain her side of the story. She said that doing that would help her have closure. Edward agreed. He promised her that he would call her as soon as he got back in town so they could have coffee together.

He had a good walk. When he reached Lady, he felt at complete peace. He kneeled in front of her and closed his eyes. He felt one with her. He kept repeating, "I am here, I am here, I am here." He didn't know why he wanted to say those words. He just wanted to be in the moment with the tree. He wanted to stop thinking about who he was and what he was supposed to do. He wanted to let go of the thought that he had just let go of Lily. He had made that choice. He wanted now to be free of it. He kept repeating, "I am here." He stopped saying the words, then began to think them, to imagine them so intensely that he suddenly heard them emanating from within himself. He wasn't alone. Who was this new "I" that was here? Was it Edward himself? Was it his higher self? Was it the tree? Was it the little angel he had seen in his dreams? Was it God? He only knew that he wasn't alone. He was part of everything and everything was part of him.

He wished he could see the angels. He wished he could be sleeping and dreaming, but he couldn't. He stood up, said goodbye to the gigantic tree, and walked away. As he wandered along the path toward the house, he thought about Sara and her letters. How did this woman believe so much in a God that she couldn't see? How could people be so sure of their particular religious practice? He didn't understand, yet he knew from his own life experiences that he couldn't deny a higher force of some kind. There had been too many times when his life path had been changed for it to be a coincidence. He felt not only safe but loved to be able to contact a higher force through his thoughts and meditations and ask for help. When the recent events of his life began to unfold, he hadn't thought to ask for help—not as he walked to his boss's office, not after he lost his job, not even after he lost Lily. He only knew that for a long time he had felt insignificant. His job didn't matter to people. Anyone else could do it. He didn't matter that much to anyone in particular either, since his mother died. He was beginning to understand that he was also insignificant to Lily. She saw him only through her own needs, not for the man he was. He was completely replaceable for her. If he'd become sick and needed someone to take care of him, he would have been alone.

The move to Little Falls had changed all that. He felt significant. He meant something to Max, and now to Kate, not only as friends but maybe someday as family. He had a purpose. He needed to understand why he was chosen to find Sara's letters. What was there in Sara's life that connected her to him? He was excited to see what her next letter would be about, to watch her life unfold through those letters. His steps grew faster and stronger, along with an urge to live his life with purpose. What was his purpose? He was going to go to the house and talk to Max.

When Edward arrived, Max was walking outside in the driveway, using his cane. "Hi there, Sir Major," Edward yelled.

"Hello, Ed, did you have a good walk?"

"Yes sir, it was wonderful. I even had a talk with Lily."

"That's great. Nothing is really worthy of your fear. You need to face your fears if you want them to become smaller. When you're afraid of doing something without a real reason, you feed your fear and make it grow that much stronger. There's only one way to face your fears, and that is face on. Remember, Edward, every time you do something that you fear but know deep inside you have to do, you become bigger than your fear. You do look taller to me now, anyways." The men laughed.

That night Edward dreamt about the little angels again. In his dreams he tried to recognize the one particular angel that had communicated with him when he was sleeping under the gigantic tree. The little angels were flying up and down in a room in front of a large golden door. Edward was curious where this door led to. He walked toward it and touched the knob. The little angels didn't seem to care about Edward's actions. They were just flying around and playing and giggling like little children. As he touched the doorknob, one of the angels lit on top of his hand.

Edward's eyes locked onto those of the little guy and he suddenly recognized him. *Hello, my little friend,* Edward thought. He could hear his own voice inside his chest as he thought the words. This was the second time that he had experienced this. It was very empowering to him.

"Hello, Edward Evans, where do you want to go?" the little angel asked.

"Where does this door open to?" Edward asked, intensely curious.

"It will open to wherever you want to go," the angel responded.

"I'd like to see my mother." Edward wasn't sure if his request was even reasonable.

In a monotone voice, the little angel said, "Open the door, Edward Evans. You can go and see your mother."

Edward pushed down the knob and the door opened effortlessly. As he looked inside he was overwhelmed with the amount of light that was flowing toward him. He stepped in. He was walking in an open space into a place that he couldn't have imagined. He saw a wooden bridge in front of him. As he walked onto the bridge, all he could see around was blue sky and some clouds. He looked down and saw that the bridge was in a field of deep green grass. He knew that the bridge was there to show him the way. So he followed the path. Suddenly he saw a house with a violet door in front of him. He got chills, knowing that his mother must be inside. He walked eagerly to the door and knocked.

The woman who opened the door didn't resemble his mother. She looked to be in her fifties, tall and slender, with dark brown eyes and short brown hair. She wore a white tee-shirt and pants and appeared to be waiting for him. "Hello, Eddie, come in. How are you? You look wonderful. Your mother is waiting for you." Smiling sweetly, she placed her hand on his shoulder and directed him inside.

As Edward stepped inside, he was shocked by the aroma of homemade cookies that his mother used to bake for him at Christmas. His eyes filled with tears of joy as he walked through a hallway to a large room with large, comfortable sofas and a table in the center that had a large silver plate filled with his mother's homemade cookies. He picked up one and sat on a sofa. As he bit into the cookie, its taste and smell took him back to his childhood as if it was today. Suddenly he realized that it tasted and smelled like the cookie he bought from the boy who came to his apartment and sold him the newspaper. Could there possibly be a connection?

He sat comfortably on the sofa and waited to see his mother. Looking around, he saw the room's light neutral-colored walls and the high ceiling full of skylights that kept the room well lit and warm. A large window overlooking a green open space had interesting drapery: the material looked just like grass, with large, colorful flowers seemingly growing from it.

Suddenly Edward heard his mother's voice calling him. "Eddie honey, come on over here please." He stood up and followed her voice. He went back to the hallway and opened a door that took him to the kitchen, where he saw his mother holding her special lemonade in a large glass. She looked just like always when she was cooking in the kitchen. Wearing a summer dress with a flower pattern, she looked the way he remembered her when he was ten. When she saw him, she placed the lemonade glass on the kitchen counter and opened her arms to her son. Edward ran to her and hugged her. Her hair smelled like the honey shampoo she always used. He never wanted to let her go. "I miss you, Mom."

"Eddie, my darling, I am with you. I have never left you. Can't you see that? You're doing so well, I'm so proud of you."

Edward looked at his mother disbelievingly. "Come on, Mom, you know that I'm a mess. I lost Lily and my job. I'm foolishly wasting time reading letters from someone named Sara, who asked that God let them be found by a special person. Well, I'm the one who found them, but I don't have a clue why God would think me special. I'm sure there are more qualified people in this world who could make better use of them. Why did it have to be me? I don't understand…I can't seem to do anything right…I can't even figure out what to do with my own life. How am I going to take responsibility for this woman's letters? I'm just not good enough," Edward cried.

Edward's mother always knew how to make Edward feel better. She wiped his tears away with a napkin, then asked him to follow her. They walked toward the front door. She opened it for them, and they stepped outside onto a small porch where a swing hung to the left. On it sat the woman who had earlier opened the entrance door for Edward. His mother looked at her. "Sara honey, we need your help over here. Edward has some doubts about being the one who found your letters. Can you talk with him?"

Sara got up from the swing and followed Edward's mother to the family room. Happy and excited, Edward followed the women. He couldn't believe that the same day that he had a chance to see his mother again, he also saw Sara. How did these women know each other?

They sat together on one of the comfortable sofas, Edward next to his mother, holding her hand. He held onto her as if he could keep her from ever going away. He hadn't shown so much emotion toward anyone since she died. He felt so much previously hidden emotion that he didn't know what to do with it. He looked at Sara in disbelief. There she was, sitting in front of him. He felt as if he knew her in so many ways, yet was uncertain if she was happy that he was the one to have found her letters. Edward's mother asked Sara to explain to him how she felt about Edward being the chosen one.

Sara looked straight at Edward with a sweet smile and said, "Dear Edward, I didn't know who was going to find my letters. Thank you for taking on the task. You are a blessing in my world. I heard the concerns you shared with your mother. I could hear them in my heart as you felt them. When I was living on earth, I too had so many doubts about my abilities. I could never believe what I know now. I just couldn't understand my oneness with everything and everyone. You are there now and you will come to terms with everything that you will learn and experience. You will come to know in your heart that whatever you decide to do with those letters will be fine."

Edward interrupted, "But such an important thing—your letters. You've been waiting so long for someone to find them; they shouldn't have been found by me. I can assure you of that. I'm confused. I don't know what to do with them when I'm done reading them. Max and Kate are leaving it up to me to decide what to do with them. They keep telling me that since I'm the one who found your letters, I'm the one to read them, and I'm sure they'll not help me decide what to do with them."

Sara moved closer to Edward on the couch and said, "Dear Eddie, don't you see? It won't make any difference to me one way or another what you do with those letters. They are part of your lessons now. I left them there for you. I didn't know who I left them for at the time, but I just had a strong desire to write them and leave them. I did what I had to do. The rest is up to you. Whatever you do with them is fine with me. Just remember that we are always connected to each other. We are one with everything. I was pushed by a force inside me to write and hide the letters. The same force that pulled you out of your comfortable apartment and took you to the woods to Max had pushed me. Max's little house was pushing him to place that ad that pulled you in to fix his porch. Everything is connected, Eddie. You don't have to understand it. So as far as I'm concerned, I'm done with that lifetime. I'm content with everything that I've accomplished and learned. Even though it doesn't matter to me what you do with the letters, I'm very excited to see what unfolds. It's all up to you, Eddie. I am no longer there. I cannot tell you how happy I am to meet you. I could never imagine in my wildest dreams who would find my letters. But God always amazes us with miracles." Sara stood up, excused herself, and walked out of the room with an indescribable grace about her. Edward was relieved to know that he couldn't harm her by whatever he decided about her letters. He was at peace now.

Looking at his mother with continued wonder, he asked her how she knew Sara. His mother responded, "You know Sara through her letters. I know Sara through you. I told you that I am with you. Even though I'm not physically with you, I can feel you every time you think of me. I will always be your mother as long as you are in this lifetime and need me as a mother."

"Where is Dad?" Edward asked.

"Do you want to see him, Eddie?" she asked gently.

"Yes, of course. I want to see him. Where is he?"

Edward's mother continued, "I promise that you will see him. It's hard for you to understand this dimension. He's not here now, but I will bring him to you. He's so proud of the way you worked on that porch. He thinks you did a far better job than he would have done." She smiled.

"I'm not so sure that I believe that, Mom. But I'll take that compliment any day. I don't want to leave you. Can I just be here with you?" Edward asked.

"You have your life to live. You have all of your lessons to learn. You have so much joy and so much living to do. You have plenty of time to be here. You are needed where you are, Eddie. You'll be fine. I'm so very proud of you, my darling."

Edward felt that his time with his mother was up, that she was saying good-bye to him. He stood up and hugged her again. Once again he smelled her hair and tried to remember how it made him feel. She walked him to the door with a smile, trying to hold back her tears so he wouldn't be sad. He knew how his mother felt. "I will see you soon," Edward told her.

As he walked out of the room, he consciously held a picture of this place in his memory, hoping he could return any time he needed to see her. The narrow bridge was right in front of him. He crossed it and was soon in front of the golden door. He grasped the knob, opened the door, and walked inside. The little angels were flying in the room and giggling. He looked at the bed and saw that the little angel that had shown him the door was sitting on top of the pillow. He opened a window, thinking that he could use some fresh air. He lay down on the bed and watched the little angel jump up and down on him.

"Thank you for that," Edward told the little angel.

"I am here, Edward Evans. Anytime you need me, I am here." Edward closed his eyes to rest. He felt the little angel jump up and down on him.

CHAPTER TEN

Edward opened his eyes to see a little bird sitting on top of his nose. The bird had come in through the open window by the side of the bed. With a smile, he got up slowly so as not to scare it. He remembered all of the details in his dream, including opening the window. But he couldn't explain how the actual window, which had been closed when he fell asleep, had come to be opened. He went downstairs and took a long, warm shower, shaved, and got ready for his day. Max had gone for his morning walk. Edward started to make breakfast for everyone, since Kate was soon to join them. He kept thinking about his dream. It was so vivid he wasn't sure if it was a dream. He just knew in his heart that he had seen his mother and he had seen Sara.

He had finished making the French toast when Max and Kate walked in together. "Good morning, guys," Edward cried out cheerfully.

"Good morning," they responded.

Kate looked at him. "Edward, what's happened? You look so happy!"

"Nothing, I saw my mother and Sara last night. I now know what Sara looks like," Edward said with a smile.

Kate looked right at Edward. "Now I'm jealous! I want to see Sara too. Please tell us exactly what she looks like." Max nodded. They sat around the table while eating French toast and listened to Edward tell all about his dream.

Max listened very carefully, tearing up by the time Edward had finished his story. Max placed his hand on Edward's shoulder. "Son, I am so happy that you chose to come here and fix this porch. I am beginning to feel that I am accomplishing most of the things that I was supposed to do without my wife."

"No way, sir," Edward replied. "My part of the story is just beginning, and I know that you're supposed to play a part for a long time. You'll be here for quite a while, sir."

Max smiled. He appreciated Edward's caring thoughts. He knew he'd found a good friend.

"So everyone, are you ready for another letter from Sara?" Edward asked. When Max and Kate nodded in agreement, Edward picked up Sara's letters and began reading the next one.

Dear God,

I am saddened by Mr. Howard's death. A lot of people had many good things to say about him. I feel bad for Mrs. Howard. She looked pretty upset at her husband's funeral. She kept talking to Paul. I don't blame her for not wanting to talk with me. She must have felt that I have had doubts about her. I am so sorry about what I thought. I am glad that I listened to Paul and quit with my talks about her. Paul is going to go to her house next week. She told him that she needs his help with some of Mr. Howard's paperwork. Paul told me that he doesn't want to charge her this one time. He said that he will charge her if she needs something permanent. I am so proud of Paul for being so kind and generous. I asked him to ask Mrs. Howard to come over to our house for supper. I hope she accepts my invitation. Helen and Jane still don't like Mrs. Howard. I know they are young and they believe what they want to believe. I'm not going to force them to like her, but I already told them that they should be respectful. They said they understand. They are such good girls. I thank you, God, for all of my blessings.

> Here is a little something for the heavens.
> Little angel, little man with wings,
> Are you from heaven? Or do you belong to earth?
> Do you like this house? Or is it just me?
> Are you everyone's or do you belong just to me?
> I see you sometimes in my dreams,
> I hear you giggling with such peace.
> Are you from heaven? Or do you belong to earth?

With Loving Respect,
Sara

When Edward finished, the short poem continued running through his mind. He told Max and Kate that Sara was probably talking about the same little angel that he kept seeing in his dreams. Max and Kate had no answers for Edward. They all just sat there quietly, each thinking about this unique experience.

Edward put Sara's letter on the kitchen table and said, "I wish I could see that golden door whenever I wanted. It was a humbling experience, guys. Why do we have to die to reach that level?"

Kate looked at him. "Well, you for one look alive to me, and you've already seen what you have seen. I guess this proves that you don't have to be dead to see it. Am I right?"

Max nodded. "I agree with Kate, but what I'd like to know is why Edward can be here in the flesh and see all of this but we can't. I'm positive that we're part of this story too." Later Edward took Max for his doctor's appointment while Kate went home. They were all to meet again the next day to continue with Sara's next letter.

The following day started early. Edward was hyper. He was eager to find out how Sara's life was turning out. Kate and Edward sat around the kitchen table waiting for Max to return from his morning walk. Kate finished making a fresh pot of coffee, poured some for Edward, and commented, "I'm going to agree with Helen and Jane on Mrs. Howard's guilt. I do think she had something to do with her husband's death."

Edward couldn't disagree more. "You can't judge her that way. Even Sara is sorry that she was suspicious of Mrs. Howard. Besides, this is real life, not a murder mystery. I think those women speculated like that just to make their lives a little exciting. Even though Sara felt sorry for even thinking about things like that, I think it was only innocent gossip."

Getting up to pour herself another cup of coffee, Kate replied, "I want to point out to you that after her husband's death, Mrs. Howard approached only Paul, not Sara. Why should she want to get close to Sara's husband all of the sudden? Especially since she used to say that Sara was too good for Paul. Say it to Sara herself.

The whole thing sounds fishy to me. I think Sara was just a very simple, trusting woman, but I have a different view."

"But Kate, I know that in your experience your employer had plans to kill his wife, but back in those times this Mrs. Howard wouldn't have had much motive."

"Let's see how the story unfolds. I'm still very suspicious." Kate opened the door and walked out to the porch. "I'm beginning to worry about Max. He's using a cane and shouldn't be going too far. What do you say we go after him?"

"Sounds good to me."

The two of them set out on the path that Max usually took for his morning walks. "Are you going to see Lily when you go back?" Kate asked.

Edward was taken by surprise. He didn't want to answer the question, but he had to tell Kate the truth. "Yes, I am. She called me. I told her that we are over, but I don't think she believes me. I promised to meet with her and we would talk. Do you think I'm making a mistake?"

Kate stopped and looked at Edward. "Look, Ed, you know that you're the only one who can answer that question. I'm sorry if I asked you so directly. Maybe it isn't even my business. Let's just forget about it."

"I admit I was caught off guard by your question, but I'm glad that you brought it up. I don't know if I can sit face-to-face with Lily and be as strong as I feel now. It's easier to talk to her over the phone. I mightn't be able to do the right thing when I see her in person."

"Then it's very important for you to see each other. You must see her. You're not done with your lesson until you pass your test. Whatever you decide will be fine, Ed. But you already know that," Kate said with a reassuring smile. Edward really liked the ease with which he could talk with Kate. She understood his position.

As they resumed walking, they kept calling Max, but he seemed to be nowhere to be found. Kate suggested that he might have seen a friend on his way and changed his plans. But after more discussion, they concluded that Max wouldn't trade his morning walk to spend time with anyone. Besides, it was already past the time when he had promised to meet them. They continued their search for some time and still couldn't find Max. Now Edward was really worried. Max couldn't have gone too far with his cane. They decided to go separate ways and come back to the same point within an hour. The sun was beginning to warm up the day and Max didn't like walking when it got too warm. Edward decided to go to the gigantic tree. Maybe Max had decided that he wanted to rest in its shade.

As Edward approached the tree, he saw the shadow of someone lying close to it. He ran to it and found Max lying facedown by the roots. "Max, are you OK? What happened?"

He turned him over and checked his breathing. Thankfully he was breathing. Next he checked Max's pulse. It was weak. "Answer me, Max. What happened?"

Max began to respond, speaking in a very weak voice, "Something fell on me as I was walking. I think it was a branch from an old tree. My head hurts."

Edward noticed that the left side of Max's head had a little blood on it. He told Max to rest and not to worry about anything. He desperately called Kate with his cell phone and was relieved to find enough reception to connect them. Kate knew exactly where the tree was. She told him to stay there and she would bring help.

Edward tried to keep Max talking. He didn't know what else to do. He was afraid to move Max around, so he just tried to keep him comfortable. He was worried about serious head injury.

It was a bewildering day for Edward. Kate had managed to call their local sheriff department for help. Their emergency unit sped to the location of the old tree and transferred Max back to the town hospital. It turned out that a heavy tree branch had fallen on Max as he was walking. He managed to walk himself to Lady, where he thought he'd be easier to find, since everyone, including Edward and Kate, knew her location and her meaning for him. Later in the hospital, when Max was alone with Edward and Kate, he told them that he heard his wife's voice telling him to walk to the tree. He recognized her voice, which kept him going until he reached Lady's trunk. Max had tears in his eyes when he spoke of his late wife. Even though he hadn't seen her, her voice was enough to take him back to the time that they were together.

Edward and Kate were the only people who understood Max. "I told you that you still have a long time to be around. Even your wife knows it. Why don't you quit doing dangerous things and give yourself a little rest until the foot, and now your head, are healed?" Edward pleaded.

When the nurse came in with the good news of no internal bleeding, they were all relieved. Jokingly Max warned his friends that he had read in a book somewhere that whatever happened once wouldn't happen again, but whatever happened twice would always happen the third time. Since he already had injured his foot and his head, he warned his friends that one more might be on its way. Kate couldn't believe Max would say something so cruel and unfair at a time like this. Edward just laughed and told Max to please take it easy and have his last accident at the house and to please not injure himself too much since Sara's letters were waiting for them.

A few days later they settled in and continued the reading with Sara's next letter. Max sat on the couch with a cast on his foot and a bandage around his head. Before Edward started to read Sara's next letter, he asked Max to stay still and not to get himself in trouble for a moment so they could see what was happening with Sara's life. Max promised his friends not to hurt himself for the duration of the day. Max and Edward laughed but Kate shook her head. "Men can sometimes laugh at things that aren't even funny."

Edward continued to read...

CHAPTER ELEVEN

Dear God,

When Paul went to Mrs. Howard's house to help her with her late husband's papers, he came home furious and wouldn't tell me what happened. He told me not to worry about it and that Mrs. Howard wouldn't be bothering us anymore. I don't understand what could have happened. I cannot imagine why Paul all of a sudden dislikes Mrs. Howard so much. Helen and Jane tell me that their father must be suspecting Mrs. Howard of poisoning her late husband. But I told the girls not to talk about things like that. I am sure if that was the case, Paul would have said something to me. Anyway, there is nothing that I can do now. I pray for everyone to be fine. I will give Paul some time and maybe he will tell me what happened when he is ready. I will talk this over with Jessie next time that I see her. Maybe she can figure this out better than I can. Maybe Paul will say something to Jessie's husband and then I can figure out what happened.

I guess I have to keep my curiosity under control for now. I just want to know the truth. I don't understand why Paul doesn't trust me enough to open up to me. I will pray that soon he will change his mind. I cannot help but think of what could have happened there at Mrs. Howard's house. What if Mrs. Howard was rude to Paul? Maybe in front of her help. Maybe she accused him of something, but what? She must have done something awful for Paul to act this way. He rarely gets upset like this. I wish I could hear the truth from Paul himself. Maybe if I sleep, I can dream about what really happened. It would feel better if Paul just told me himself.

> Here is a little something for the heavens.
> Some say this, some say that.
> Day says light, night says dark.
> Who is right? Who is wrong?
> Time goes up, then goes down.
> I grew up, I'll grow down.
> I live up, my rights and wrongs.
> (I don't understand this line.)
> I don't know what's really right.
> I will know right from wrong,
> Someday.

With Love and Respect,
Sara

Filled with curiosity, Kate asked Max and Edward what they thought happened between Paul and Mrs. Howard. Max thought that whatever it was it couldn't have been about Mr. Howard's death. Edward agreed. He argued that Mrs. Howard couldn't have been clever enough to kill her husband and later be stupid enough to admit it to Paul. He couldn't believe that Mrs. Howard had any reason to confess unless she'd completely lost her mind. Kate was dying for Edward to read another letter. Max had no objections.

Edward continued.

Dear God,

I can't believe that I have been so naïve. Helen and Jane, who are barely fourteen, knew better than me what Mrs. Howard was capable of doing. Jessie told me that Mrs. Howard had asked for help from the husband of the lady who owns the woman's clothing store, then threw herself at him. That made everything clear. I cannot believe that I didn't see that coming. I am so blind to everything that goes on around me. That is why she wanted me not to do much for my husband, so she would have a better chance to seduce Paul. Last night I told Paul everything, insisting that he tell me if that was what happened when he went to her house. He nodded sadly, telling me later that he didn't want to hurt me. I didn't talk to him for the rest of the night. I am very upset. Paul should have told me the truth. I know that he did what any honorable man in his position would have done: leave her house and tell her off, but he should have told me what happened. I am his wife and he should share these things with me. I deserve a better explanation. What about Mrs. Howard herself? How can anyone be this way? Why did she marry her husband if she didn't love him? I cannot imagine how she is going to face the people of this town now, after what she has done. I am just so disappointed in her. Here I was feeling sorry for her since she had lost her husband, and at the same time she was doing all that. I hope that I can find it in my heart to forgive her someday. I just don't want to think about forgiving her tonight. I am too upset with her to think about forgiveness.

I didn't write much for the heavens this time, only one line:

The only way out of the dark hole is to light a fire of truth. You might burn your fingers holding the fire, but you will see your way out of the hole.

With Love and Respect,
Sara

Kate felt righteous. "Sara has the right to be upset with her husband. I would feel the same way if I were in her shoes." Edward didn't comment, lying low and grateful that Kate didn't say, "I told you so."

As Kate walked over to see if Max needed anything, Edward's cell phone started to ring. Lily's number appeared on the screen. He excused himself and went outside on the porch to talk to her in private. "Hello?" Edward answered.

"Hi, Ed, I have to see you. My dad had a heart attack, please come," Lily announced, breaking into tears.

Shocked, Edward told her that he would come right away. Returning inside, Edward informed Max and Kate that he had to see Lily because her father just had a heart attack. Max understood and wished him a safe trip. Edward promised to return to finish Sara's letters. He went upstairs to pack, leaving his tools because he knew that he would return to Little Falls. As he passed them on his way out, he called out, "Please be safe, Major. I need you to keep yourself in shape until I come back. No more danger-ous adventures for now."

Max assured him that everything was going to be fine and that Edward should just concentrate on doing what he had to do. Kate also said good-bye, but not much more. She didn't even come out of the house to see him leave, but made herself busy changing Max's head bandage.

Edward was conflicted about seeing Lily. He wanted to make a clean break from her, yet during the long trip he kept telling himself that he was doing the right thing in seeing her. They had been engaged for a long time, so the least he could do was to con-sole her at a time like this. He wanted to remain friends who could count on each other in difficult times. Four hours later, he arrived at his apartment. He was surprised to find it clean and spotless, since he had left it in a mess. He went inside the bedroom to find the bed done with sheets that had been washed and ironed. His clothes were neatly stacked together in their respective drawers. He was furious at Lily for this intrusion. He remembered that he had placed his mother's ring inside his leather jacket's pocket. He quickly checked inside his closet and was pleased to find the ring where he had left it. He called his building's manager and asked if he could send someone right away to change the lock. Showering quickly, he called a mutual friend of his and Lily's to ask about her father's condition. He hadn't survived the attack and died in the hospital. There was to be a funeral for him the following day.

After the locksmith changed the lock, Edward dialed Lily's number. She asked him to meet her at her parents' house, where she was helping her stepmother with the many arrangements.

As he approached, he saw many cars parked along the street and in their driveway. Parking some distance away, he walked toward the house feeling numb. Lily stood outside the door waiting for him. She scanned him up and down, shocked that he looked so different. "Thanks so much for being here, Edward. I'm so glad that I don't have to go through this by myself," she said as she hugged him. He expressed his sorrow over her father's sudden death and how grief-stricken she must be. Lily nodded, took his hand, and took him inside.

Lucy was arranging flowers as Edward and Lily walked in. She opened her arms to hug him. He hugged her warmly, telling her how sorry he was. She invited him to sit down, then asked Lily to call the funeral home to check on the progress of the funeral arrangements. Lily eagerly left to make the call as Edward sat down on the couch across from Lucy.

"I'm so glad you're back with us. I always knew that you were an honorable man," Lucy continued. Edward listened in disbelief, since Lucy was the one who had told Edward not to call Lily anymore. Could the death of her husband have confused this poor woman? He couldn't blame her now. "Please, Edward, you must be around Lily now. We cannot leave her alone. I really worry about her. Since you left, she's been a different person. She's been very unhappy. I think she's realized how much you mean to her. She's such a beautiful girl. I love her like my own daughter. I do want the best for her in my heart, so I need you to be a stable support for her now. I've called your boss and arranged for you to return to work. I scheduled you to start next week, so you can be here for Lily at the funeral. Please don't thank me. Just stay close to Lily and everything will be just fine." Before Edward could respond, she got up and walked out of the room to call some people about the funeral arrangements.

Furious, Edward felt trapped. He couldn't just walk out on Lily, leaving her alone to cope with her grief. He needed time to absorb everything that was going on. If only he could talk to Max.

Actually, it might not be such a bad deal after all. He had his job back, a second chance at work he knew how to do and that threatened no surprises. He didn't have time to think. He stepped into the kitchen to see how Lily was doing. To make himself useful, he volunteered to drive to the funeral home to make sure everything was set for the next day.

Edward now saw himself at center stage. He had even written a eulogy for her father, but he abandoned the idea of reading it at the funeral since he didn't feel that he had known the father that well. His and Lily's mutual friends were all there and counting on him. Lily smiled at him every chance she got, happy just to be close to him. Later, after the funeral, Lily told him how much she had missed him. When she started to cry, he wiped her tears and held her in his arms. Everything was happening so fast that he was reduced to watching his life happening in front of him. He felt uncontrollably pulled in, not knowing how to be himself.

When he returned to his apartment that night, he realized that he hadn't asked Lily why she had taken it upon herself to clean his apartment. Though initially feeling invaded, he now didn't care too much about it. There was no harm done. So she had someone clean his apartment. Big deal. Why was he being so unreasonable about everything? She must have cared a lot about him to have done that. At a time when she had just lost her father, she had thought to do something nice for him. Glad that he hadn't said anything to Lily, he was determined to thank her later.

That night Edward had another vivid dream. He sat in his armchair, the little angel on his lap. However, though usually happily playing and giggling around him, the little angel was now looking at him sadly. "What's the matter, little guy?" Edward asked. As in the other vivid dreams, Edward's mouth wasn't moving, but he could hear his voice inside his chest very loudly.

The angel replied, "I'm not free to play around. You keep ignoring me."

"I'm not ignoring you, little guy. I'm your friend. Tell me what's wrong with you and I'll help you."

A bit impatiently, the angel replied, "I already told you. You know exactly what's wrong. I'm not your priority. You keep ignoring my happiness."

"How do I ignore your happiness? I would ignore my own happiness over anyone else's any day. How can you say that about me?" Edward asked defensively.

"That's what I just said," the little angel desperately replied. "You ignore me. I am here. You are here. I am you, Edward Evans. I am you when you are Edward and I am you when you aren't Edward. You see me when you care about yourself, and you don't see me when you ignore yourself. You aren't acting like my best friend anymore. I am hurt. Don't you feel hurt inside, Edward Evans?"

Edward was bewildered. What was this little guy talking about? Did he mean what he said literally? Was he Edward himself? How could Edward be a little angel? He didn't understand. "How can you be me?" Edward asked.

"I am the part of you that you choose to ignore now. I am the part that reminds you why you are here. You keep forgetting. You keep being afraid. I know that there is nothing to be afraid of, but you choose not to listen to me. You will see me happy only when you listen to yourself. Your happiness is my happiness. Do you understand, Edward Evans? Your scattered thoughts keep pushing you away from me. You get so confused. You make your world so complicated when you try to make it simple for yourself. You don't trust yourself. That is why I am sad. That is why you are sad. You have the free will to change it. Once you love yourself, you can stop being so sad. You see, your mother loving you from the other side isn't enough to make a difference for you. You have to love yourself. That is the hardest truth."

The angel jumped up from Edward's lap and started to walk around the room. Edward's eyes filled with tears. Was he hearing right? Was this little angel his higher self? Edward had read many books on the subject of the higher self but had never quite grasped the idea until now. How was putting other people's needs ahead of his own needs making him cruel toward himself? He never felt bad for putting himself in second or third place until he saw how that little angel was suffering.

Suddenly he understood that he also had a responsibility to Edward Evans. There was a part of him that needed to be loved by him. He could see how ignoring his own needs would separate him from his true being. He understood that his intuitions and feelings were meant to serve him. He had followed them before, but he had also ignored a lot of them. He understood now why he felt so miserable when he was at Lily's parents' house. He was ignoring his own needs to fulfill Lily's. He was putting Lily's desires ahead of his own. He now realized that this path felt wrong to him. This wasn't what he had signed up for. He had a right to be happy. He realized that the little angel was on his lap again, jumping up and down. "Are you excited, little guy?"

"Yes, there is so much to see and so much to learn and so much to experience." Edward stood up and opened his window to breathe in fresh air. He went right back to his bed and closed his eyes. He slept comfortably, confident that everything was going to be fine.

Next morning he woke up with vivid memories of his dream. He saw that the window beside his armchair was opened. He closed the open window and called Max, who told him not to worry about anything, to stay as long as he needed to finish what he had to do. It always made Edward feel good to talk to Max. Edward asked how Kate was doing. Max reported that she was OK, but suggested that Edward call and ask her himself. Edward agreed, but his call went right to her voice mail. He left her a message, saying that he wanted to see how she was doing and that he would call her later. He also said that he had some things to take care of, but he would later return to Little Falls to finish Sara's letters.

Edward called his old office and asked to speak to Gregg. Told that he was unavailable, Edward left a message on his voice mail. "Hi, Gregg, this is Edward Evans. I heard from Lucy Jones that she made arrangements for you to reinstate my old job. I'm very grateful to you and to Lucy for her thoughtfulness. However, Lucy didn't know that I'd made other plans, so I won't be back to my old position. I hope you didn't go to too much trouble and want to thank you again for the opportunity. Give my best to your family." At that, Edward hung up the phone and felt better than he had since he'd returned home.

He called Lily to meet him in a local coffee shop where they had often gone before. He chose a table in the corner, where they would have more privacy. The hostess seated them and took their order for drinks. "I'm so glad you're back in my life, Ed. Every-thing is the way it's supposed to be," Lily began, offering up her sweetest smile.

Before Edward had a chance to respond, his cell phone rang. It was Kate. He excused himself and walked outside the coffee shop. "Hi, Kate, I do want to talk to you, but I can't now. Can I call you later today?"

"Sure, I was just calling you back. Call me whenever you're free," Kate answered.

Edward thanked her and said good-bye. He went back inside the coffee shop and returned to his seat. "Sorry for the interruption, I had to take that call," Edward explained. Lily didn't say anything. Edward started to sip his coffee. "Lily, I'm not going back to my old job. That's not for me."

"What are you going to do, Eddie? How will you support us?"

Edward wasn't sure how to answer. He paused and then replied softly, "I don't know what I'm going to do. I actually just finished a big job out of town. I'm sure I'll be OK for a while. The pay should be fairly good."

Lily visibly relaxed. "Is that where you were? Doing a job? And here I was afraid you were partying somewhere with some old girlfriend." Astonished, Edward asked her how she could even think a thing like that. "I don't know, what's a girl to think? You left me and you didn't even say where you were going," Lily complained.

"Lily, please, I didn't leave you. You left me. I have your letter wishing me well but wanting someone different from me. I don't understand you and Lucy. You both turn things around. You know what happened."

Lily wouldn't give up. She insisted that his leaving town had more to do with their breaking up than did her letter. Edward could see no use arguing the point. "It doesn't matter what happened back then anyway. Let's discuss what we want to do now."

"That's a great idea. Do you still want to use your mother's old ring for our engagement?" Lily suggested.

Edward was flummoxed. How could she be so presumptuous? Was she confused or manipulative? "Lily, I didn't want things to be this way, but you leave me no choice. We aren't getting married. We aren't a couple. I cannot even be your friend. Did you make arrangements to have my apartment cleaned?" Edward asked.

"Of course I did. I thought you would appreciate it," Lily answered accusingly.

"Well, I don't appreciate you making such decisions after we've split. I can't believe you used your key and entered my apartment or had someone else do it without checking if I was OK with it. Lucy arranged for me to go back to work starting next week without even asking me first. Do you understand what I am talking about? Wake up! We are no longer doing things together. Enough!"

Dead still, Lily began crying. Edward pleaded with her not to, but she couldn't help herself. She stood up and told Edward that she didn't want him to call her today. He was being mean and unreasonable while she was mourning her father's death. As she walked out of the coffee shop, Edward took a deep breath.

Edward returned to his apartment to pick up a few things to take back to Little Falls. He didn't want to waste any more time. He had done what he came to do. He couldn't believe that Lily was blaming him for being cruel and mean. This woman really didn't have a clue. After gathering his belongings, he locked the door, and then remembered to call Kate. She picked up after a few rings. "Hi, sorry I couldn't talk with you; I was talking to Lily."

"It's OK. I was just calling you back. I didn't mean to disturb you."

"No, you didn't disturb me. I'm coming back right now. We need to finish reading Sara's letters."

"I'll see you then," Kate replied.

Edward said good-bye and hung up the phone. He didn't feel good about the call, but he couldn't say why. He wished he could talk to Max about it. Fortunately, he would soon. In fact, he took over five hours to reach Max's house. Exhausted, he pulled into the driveway around 7:00 p.m.

CHAPTER TWELVE

Edward walked to the door and knocked. "Come in," Max yelled. As he turned the doorknob, he remembered opening the golden door in his dream. When he entered, he saw Max standing in the kitchen cooking dinner. "Hi there, did you have a good trip?" Max asked.

"Yes sir, I did. Sorry that I had to leave so suddenly. I didn't know how else to do it," Edward said.

"No worries, son. I understand. You have to answer when life calls you. You always have to choose something over something else." Edward was glad that Max understood. He told Max that he was going to take a shower and would join him for dinner.

Max had baked some potatoes with his way of making simple things taste good. As Edward began eating, he asked if Kate was going to join them. "No, Ed, she won't be joining us. She's decided to leave Little Falls for a while. A small town like this can be boring for a young woman like Kate. She came here a few years ago because she needed to be away from a lot of things. Now she feels she can handle things better and wants to get back to her life."

"But doesn't she want to hear Sara's letters?" Edward asked.

"I'm sure she'll call me and ask me about them later. You see, you're the one who found the letters. You're the one who saw Sara in your dreams. Sara told you that finding the letters and doing whatever you want with them is up to you. Her letters are meant for you, not Kate," Max reminded him.

Edward didn't like Max's answer. Max was right, but Kate was interested in the letters too. Or was she just pretending to be interested? Edward wasn't sure whether to be angry or just disappointed. "I thought she cared enough to stick around until Sara's letters were finished," Edward commented.

"What difference would that make?" Max asked.

Edward had no answer. He didn't know why the news upset him so. He was angry at Kate for leaving in the middle of everything. They had shared so much together. She had seemed genuinely interested in the letters and pleased with the three of them sharing them together, yet suddenly she just decided to pick up and leave. How inconsiderate. She hadn't even called him to say good-bye.

That night Edward couldn't sleep. He thought about all the things that Lily had told him that day and the phone call with Kate. Maybe he shouldn't have picked up the phone when Kate called. Maybe he shouldn't have told Kate the truth about where he was and what he was doing. All he did was tell the truth and he managed to ruin everything. He didn't know how to react to anything. He was even mad at Sara for writing those letters in the first place and placing him in such an awful position. He tossed and turned all night.

He waited for the sun to come up so he could go downstairs to join Max on his morning walk. Max had already washed up and was ready to go. "If you give me five minutes, I'll wash up and join you," Edward requested.

"I'll be here," Max genially responded.

Edward and Max walked down their usual path. Edward liked feeling the cold of the chilly morning air. Max was using his cane now. His doctor had opened his cast and given him a special boot to wear, which was easier to walk in than the cast. They were going slow since Max had to stop and rest every ten minutes or so. "Why are you so upset with yourself, son?" Max asked. "Why don't you enjoy the beautiful scenery?"

"I'm not sure if I deserve to enjoy any good moments now. I don't like my own company," Edward answered.

"What don't you like about yourself?" Max asked.

"I don't understand how I pushed Kate away by being honest." As soon as his comment was out of his mouth, Edward regretted it. He didn't want to admit to Max, or to himself for that matter, that his anger had anything to do with Kate's leaving.

Max smiled kindly. "Everyone sees reality through their own eyes. You're looking at the story from only your own point of view. Let's try to see Kate's point of view."

Edward objected, "I was trying to tell Lily that I couldn't be with her when Kate called me. So I picked up the phone and told her that I would call her back. Later, after Lily left when she was done accusing me of being a mean and thoughtless person, I called Kate back and told her that I was talking to Lily when she had called.

That's the whole story. How can I see it differently from Kate's point of view?"

Max explained, "Your story makes sense if Kate was indifferent toward you. She wouldn't care one way or another who you were with or what you were saying to her. But if, and only if, Kate had any feelings for you, then she would have heard that the man she had some feelings for had to run to his ex-fiancée's rescue when her father had a heart attack. And then he had to talk with the ex-fiancée and couldn't talk to another woman in front of her. Why couldn't this man pick up the phone and freely talk to her? Why couldn't he unless he cared what his ex-fiancée thought of him talking to another woman?"

Max had a good point. Edward hadn't thought about it from that angle. Kate could possibly like him. And now he had ruined any chance that he ever had with her. He felt sick to his stomach. "I messed up, Major," Edward continued. "I had a good thing and ruined it. I kept thinking that Kate was there only to listen to Sara's letters. I didn't see that she cared for me."

Max looked him directly in the eye. "Well, let's see, you can feel sorry for yourself or you can do something about it. What do you want to do, Edward?"

"I want to have a chance with Kate," Edward firmly replied.

"OK then. When we go back, make it your mission to explain yourself to Kate. She isn't an easy person to persuade, but you never know until you try. I've known Kate years longer than you have, so take my advice and open up to her. She can handle it." Max smiled. Edward felt so much better. Only a few minutes of talk with this man transformed his thinking and emotional state. Yes, he would ask Kate for another chance. He would explain to her that this was just a misunderstanding.

As they walked back, Max kept stopping and gasping for air. Beginning to worry about him again, Edward asked him not to walk so fast. Suddenly Max stopped and let go of his cane. He placed his hands to his chest and began breathing heavily.

"Are you OK, Max? What is happening? What can I do for you?" Edward yelled, starting to panic.

"I think I'm having a heart attack. I'm not sure what to do."

Edward couldn't believe his ears. Just back from funeral arrangements for a man he barely knew, a man whom he dearly cared for was having a heart attack: two events over which he had no control. He dialed 911 for help. The two of them were close enough to Max's driveway that Edward could easily describe their location. He helped Max lie down on the grass, constantly reassuring him that help was on its way. "Max, it's your fault that I'm in this position. You haven't even paid me for remodeling your porch yet. You better pull through this one. I won't let you do this to me, man." Max smiled faintly at Edward, who continued, "Stay with me, Max. I need you. Think of Sara's letters. We have to finish them. Your wife wants you to live your life here. Please, Max, just stay with me a little longer."

The emergency crew arrived after what seemed an eternity. They took Max in the ambulance while Edward followed in his car. He called Kate and left her a message. "Hi, Kate, it's Edward. I'm here in Little Falls. We think Max just had a heart attack. They're taking him to the hospital. I'm so sorry that I have to leave you a message like this. Anyway, I'm going to the hospital now. Call me and I'll let you know what's happening with him as soon as I know more. I need you here. OK...bye."

Edward sat in the hospital waiting room watching the clock, trying not to think about anything bad that could happen. He couldn't get himself to watch television. There were no phone calls from Kate or anyone else. How did he get here from where he had been the day that he had lost his old job? He couldn't have then imagined being in this place. So much had changed in his life and in himself. Max had taught him so much wisdom. On the other hand, he recalled Max's comment about things happening in threes. Nonsense, of course: selective memory or coincidence. Yet Max had an eye for a lot of things. He liked that Max respected Sara's letters so much. He recalled all that Max had told him about Kate. If he had been much younger when he had met Max, he could have learned so much more from him. He couldn't think of losing Max.

Edward still futilely wondered why he was chosen to read Sara's letters and if he really saw Sara's face in his dreams. He was too tired to think about it anymore today. He remembered that he had stayed awake the night before. Yes, he could use a little sleep. He closed his eyes and started to dream.

He saw himself sitting in the waiting room chair. A woman came toward him. He seemed to recognize her face, but he couldn't tell where he had seen her before. She wore a long purple dress and had dark curly hair around her shoulders. She was very beautiful. She walked up and sat on the chair next to him. "Edward dear, are you OK? I was worried about you," she said.

"Do I know you?" Edward asked.

"I'm Beth, Max's wife." Then Edward remembered her from the picture that Max had shown him. She was even more beautiful in person. He didn't understand why he was talking to her. "How is Max doing?" Edward asked. "I'm worried about him."

"I'm here to talk to you about him. You needn't worry about him; he's done with his lessons. He's not in any pain now. He's in a better place. You are a very good friend to him. You will always be connected to us, Edward."

Beth's voice was very comforting, but Edward didn't want to hear what Beth was telling him. He started to cry. "Please let me talk to him. I still have a lot to learn from him. He's like a father to me. I can't let him go just yet."

Beth wiped Edward's tears with a white cloth. "Dear Edward, I promise you that everything will be fine. You know that after we pass through this life we aren't done. You know that we go to a better place. You've seen too much to deny it."

"Why couldn't Max come and tell me himself?" Edward asked, trying to stop crying.

"He isn't used to this transition. He's new to this. Later, when he remembers what he needs to remember, he will contact you when you ask. Please trust me, Edward. I am here for you." As soon as Beth was done speaking, she got up and walked away. Edward buried his face in hands and continued to weep.

A familiar voice called his name. "Edward, please wake up." As he opened his eyes, he saw the nurse looking at him. He knew what she was going to say. After she finished giving him the news of Max's death, she asked if she could get him anything. "Yes, some water, please," Edward asked. Later the nurse told him that they would keep Max's body overnight until his funeral arrangements could be made. He nodded and walked to his car. He didn't know how Max wanted to be buried, but he knew that it didn't matter to Max now. Whatever Edward would do, he was doing for himself.

The next morning, he decided to go to the hospital and ask about the funeral arrangements. As he walked into the hospital, he saw Kate sitting in the waiting room. He was relieved that he didn't have to make all of the decisions by himself. He was also glad to see Kate. Her eyes were puffy and red. Apparently she had arrived at the hospital very early in the morning and had heard the news. Edward opened his arms and gave her a warm hug. They held each other and cried, sharing the pain of losing Max. Edward felt his pain lessening as he cried in Kate's arms.

The hospital administrator walked over and introduced herself. "You must be Edward and Kate," she guessed. "When Max was admitted last time for his broken ankle, he signed papers giving both of you full permission to make decisions for him in the event that he wasn't able to make decisions for himself. I know this is a hard time for you, but please follow me and I will explain to you your options for caring for the body."

Edward and Kate didn't mention that they had no idea what Max wanted. They both knew that whatever they decided was for their own sakes.

The simple funeral was a peaceful event. Many of the people from Little Falls attended to pay their last respects to him. During that time, Kate stayed in her old place while Edward remained at Max's. In the morning following Max's funeral, Edward called Kate and asked to see her. They decided to go to a town restaurant and have breakfast. "I need to talk to you. I have some explaining to do," Edward said. Kate quietly listened. "I'm sorry things turned out this way, but I want you to know what happened between Lily and me."

Kate assured Edward that he didn't owe her any explanation, but he insisted. He told her the entire story: how he felt about Lily and what he did at her father's funeral. He gave her so much detail that he was surprised that he remembered it all. He described his dream in his apartment and later the one about Max's wife.

Kate wasn't surprised. She understood why he needed to empty himself. She told him that she was moved that she was someone he could share his stories with.

Edward felt lighter. Kate wasn't angry with him anymore. He thanked Max in his heart for helping him one last time with her. Kate told him that she intended to go to Max's house and gather some of his clothing to donate to the Salvation Army. "I'm sure that's what Max would have wanted," she added. Edward replied that he would see if there were any hospital bills that he had to take care of.

As Edward entered the hospital, he was directed by a clerk to the administration room. He wasn't sure what amount he could afford, but he couldn't just walk away. The hospital's administrator greeted him. "I'm Mrs. Ross. Nice to finally meet you, Mr. Evans. Sorry that we meet under such sad circumstances. Max spoke so highly of you."

"Thank you. I came to see if I can cover some of Max's expenses. I'm not a rich man, but I'll do what I can," Edward said.

"Max told me you were a man of character. I see now that he was right. You see, Mr. Evans, Max built our hospital. Before Max, our patients had to travel far to any medical facility. We are small, but we do very well for Little Falls."

Edward wondered at yet more stunning news about Max. *How did he build this hospital?* Edward thought to himself. He didn't look like a rich man. So that was why all of the people in this place respected him so much. But why would he choose to live in a small, run-down house if he had enough money to build a hospital? "I'm surprised. I had no idea of Max's generosity," Edward replied.

Mrs. Ross smiled. "There's no need to be sorry. Max was the sort of man who'd prefer not to tell people about his wealth. He donated a lot of money to this town. He helped many families in need. Everyone in Little Falls knew and respected him. We all will miss him very much."

Edward stood up, said good-bye to Mrs. Ross, then left the hospital. As he walked to his car he thought about the kind of man Max was. He missed him more than ever. How could someone be so good in every way? He thanked God for having met Max, which had changed his life forever. He also thanked Sara for writing the letters, if only because they kept him with Max longer and able to learn that much more from him.

As Edward arrived at Max's house, he was pained to see it and the porch, knowing Max would never be there. He wasn't sure if he could stay there without Max, but if he did, the only reason would be to read Sara's letters. His cell phone rang. It was Kate. "Hi, how are you?" Edward answered.

"I'm fine. What are you doing?" Kate asked.

"I was thinking about gathering my tools and leaving," Edward answered. "I don't feel comfortable staying here without Max. Did you know that he built that hospital with his own money? And here I was thinking that I needed to pay his bills. God, I really miss him."

Kate was quiet for a minute, in shock. She too had no idea that Max had money. "I don't know what to say, he was an angel. He will always be remembered. I'm coming over to help you with the cleanup. You can take Sara's letters. We both know that Max believed from the start that the letters belonged to you."

Edward knew that Kate was right. He knew that Max would have wanted him to take Sara's letters. He also knew that the only ones that he wanted to share the letters with were Max and Kate. He asked Kate if she would still want to hear Sara's letters, even though Max was gone. Kate assured him that she did. She told Edward she would be there in about an hour. They could read one or two of Sara's letters and clean up.

CHAPTER THIRTEEN

Edward was fixing a leak under the kitchen sink when Kate walked in. "Hi, what are you doing?" she asked.

"I'm trying to fix a little leak here. Max wouldn't like wasting water," Edward told her. Kate suggested that they read Sara's letters first and do the fixing and cleaning after that. Edward squirmed out from under the sink, washed his hands, grabbed the letters, joined Kate at the kitchen table, and began reading.

Dear God,

I am not sure where to start. I know that you already know about my aches and pains. Helen and Jane don't let me touch anything. They keep asking me to rest. I am not sure what use I am if I keep up this long rest. I still insist on helping them cook. But they haven't let me clean anything for a long time now.

Paul has changed so much. He keeps asking me if I need anything. Last time that I visited the doctor, he gave me some medicine for pain. It is really helpful. Thanks for all of my blessings. I am getting weak, but my life is full. I cannot write too much now, but I will write you one line.

Here is a line for your heavens.

My body can hurt as much as it can, but my heart sings with joy. There is medicine for the pains of the body, but my heart is happy and nothing compares to its ecstasy.

With Love and Respect,
Sara

Kate looked anxiously at Edward. "Wow, she must have been very ill."

Edward nodded. "I think so. I guess her husband and daughters knew her condition better than she did."

Kate added, "Maybe she didn't care about leaving this way. Maybe she felt she had everything she ever wanted. She must have been in her late fifties."

Edward was upset. He complained to Kate that it wasn't fair that Sara got sick around the same time that Max died. Since only a few more letters were left, they decided to read one more. Edward began.

Dear God,

No one in town talks about Mrs. Howard anymore. I think she is trying to live her life quietly now. I will continue to pray for her. I have already forgiven her. In my last letter, I was not sure that I could forgive her even if I tried. But my heart is clear now. I have no anger in my heart for her. I am sure you have helped me to be this way. Sometimes I am so amazed at how easily I forget to be angry at someone. I only have love in my heart. And I know that it is because of you that I am this way. Thanks again for helping me stay clear of all anger and hatred. My girls are fine too. Helen insists on learning Spanish. I am not sure what good learning Spanish does for a young woman, but she says that she loves to learn different languages, so I will support her. I think she will end up becoming a teacher, since she already loves to teach. Jane on the other hand says that her dream is to work for a newspaper company. She doesn't listen to Pauls advice that certain jobs are not made for women. I am glad that my girls are so independent at such a young age. I cannot believe that they are seventeen years old. Where did the time go?

These days I don't do much running around. I have some back pain and try to keep myself busy with more walking and less sitting. I am so blessed. Thank you for everything that I have.

Here is something for the heavens.
I have you here, my darling, I have your sweet company.
You keep my hopes alive, I keep your dreams with me.
I know how dear you are, you know how true I am.
I have you here with me, you have me near you, darling.

With Love and Respect,
Sara

Kate walked to the kitchen closet, grabbed the broom and duster, and began cleaning. Edward went back to fixing the leak under the kitchen sink. They had been busy for half an hour when some-one knocked at the door. Kate opened it to find Tom, the local sheriff, whom she knew very well. He had been a good friend to Max. He greeted her warmly and walked in. She invited him to sit on the couch and asked if he was thirsty. He asked for water. Edward stood up and greeted him. Max had introduced the two of them in town once.

"Sorry to disturb you guys, I can see that you're busy. It's a shame how suddenly we lost Max. I still can't believe it."

Edward continued Tom's thought, "I know, it's a bit crazy. We're trying to clean up and leave. I'm not comfortable staying here. Do you know if Max had any relatives that we could notify?"

Tom informed them that there were no relatives that he knew about, then added, "Actually, I'm here to tell you that last month Max took me to his attorney to witness his will. You shouldn't be in a hurry to leave this place, since he's left this house to both of you. He left a lot of his assets to different charities, but he wanted his house for the two of you."

Edward was speechless. Kate plumped down on the couch next to Tom. "Are you sure about this?" she asked.

"Positive. I know what Max wanted. I witnessed him sign his will. I'm sure you'll receive the attorney's letter in the very near future. He gave the attorney all of your information including your address-es and phone numbers. I hope you like this place as much as Max did. He was one of a kind." Tom finished his glass of water and said good-bye. He repeated his condolences for their loss and added that if they needed anything they shouldn't hesitate to contact him.

Kate couldn't get up from the couch. In a slight state of shock, she wiped the tears from her eyes. How confusing but wonderful that Max had left them this very special house. She was relieved that they did not have to rush to get out. They could take their time and make it even more wonderful than it was. Edward too was shocked and surprised. Why would Max want to leave him part of his house? They had only recently met. Though the time they spent together was powerful, it had only been several weeks. Edward didn't know what to do with this. He buried his face in his hands and tried to think through his situation. He chuckled to himself. Max hadn't paid him for his work on the porch, but left him half of this house instead. It was too much. He didn't deserve it. What made up a man like Max? It was hard for Edward to grasp a level of generosity that he had never encountered or even heard of before.

The house was now theirs. How could they ever show their gratefulness to this man? Kate looked up at the photograph of Beth above the mantle. This wonderful, generous man hadn't really left. He was placing two of his friends in a far better state than before he met them. This house would always be filled with the memories of Sara and Paul, Max and Beth, Max and Kate, Max and Edward, and Edward and Kate.

Kate wiped away her tears and stood up. Walking around the room, she asked Edward, "Could you please start to read Sara's last letter?"

Edward stood up and without saying a word picked up the stack of letters from the coffee table, took them to the kitchen, and began reading the last one.

Dear God,

I'm not planning to write another letter. I have to be able to place them where I need to. I still have some strength left in me, even though the pain is getting the better of me. Please look after Paul and my daughters. They are beautiful young women now. I wish I could see them get married. But I have Paul for that. He is the most wonderful husband that one could have asked for. I don't know what to say about my letters. They aren't much, but they are my treasures. They are a very small piece of my life. I know that you have a very special plan for them. Maybe that is why I had a strong desire to write them. Sometimes I try to imagine someone finding these letters in the future. I cannot imagine how many years it will take. I wonder what he or she will think of me when they read my writings. I guess this is a good time for me to tell this person thank you. Thank you for keeping my dream alive. There can be no mistakes. God, with you everything is perfect. Thank you.

Here are my last words for your heavens and for the special someone who finds these letters.

Time has gone: many springs, many moments.
Time for me to join those moments.
Time for me to find out your secrets.
I give you my blessings, I give you my love.
We are connected, we are one.
Take my hand whenever our meeting time and place
has come.

With Love and Respect,
Sara

Edward put down Sara's last letter. With it, Sara had addressed him as well, acknowledging their connection by thanking him. The letter had given him closure for Sara as well as for Max. He missed Max so much, missed not sharing these last letters with him. He got up, wiped his tears with a napkin, and asked Kate if she needed anything. She told him that she was fine. Sara's letters were done. Edward asked her, "Do you think Max was here with us, listening to the letters?"

"I don't know. I hope wherever he is, he's happy and free," Kate replied, to which Edward responded, "I'm sure he's just fine. His wife Beth told me that he's in a better place." Edward knew that Max would somehow listen to all of Sara's letters. For surely all three of them, even without knowing it, had promised Sara to finish them. That done, it was now up to Edward alone to do something positive with them. He had no idea yet how to fulfill that obligation, but he knew that he had to trust that special force that brought them to him to show him the way.

He asked Kate if she ever had any dreams of little flying angels. She told him that she would love to, but never had. He described how they looked, then further recounted his dreams in complete detail. When Edward finished his exhaustive account, Kate told him that she had to go back to the city early next morning to tie up some loose ends. They lapsed into an awkward silence, since both felt uncomfortable bringing up their shared ownership of the house.

Edward finally got up his courage to start. "Kate, do you want to live here? I don't mean with me, I have an apartment that I can go back to."

Relieved that Edward had broached the subject, Kate answered, "I don't think so, Edward. But I don't see why this should be a difficult situation, since we both want to live in the city. You have your apartment and I recently found a place. I would like to come here whenever I feel like it, since it isn't that long a drive. We can each take a room upstairs to use whenever we want. I'm not sure how long that can work, but for now it seems fair." Edward happily agreed with Kate's suggestion.

That night, Edward kept his own room while Kate moved into Max's. Early the next morning, Kate hurriedly prepared for her return to the city without stopping to eat breakfast. Edward got up to see her off, waiting outside until her car left the driveway. He decided to stay around Little Falls for a few more days before he went back to his apartment.

For the next few days Edward kept himself busy fixing little things around the house. He kept thinking about Max and missing him. Sometimes pretending that Max was around, he would talk out loud to him. When he decided to leave, he saw no reason now to take his tools with him. They were much more useful to him here than at his apartment. As he was driving to the city, a friend named John called to ask him what he was doing the next day. Edward told him that he didn't have any immediate plans. He wasn't sure what he was going to do for a job either, though he needed one eventually. He told John that he'd think more about that after he was well rested. When he arrived home, Edward called John to ask what he had in mind for the next day. John told him that a few of their friends wanted to get together and play pool and wondered if Edward could join them. Edward agreed to meet them at seven at a local restaurant and pool parlor.

The next evening Edward found that conversing with his old friends was sadly forced. He no longer fit with them. He kept trying to strike a spark, but wished deep down that he could just go home. Finally he told his friends that he had to leave, news that they seemed to greet with indifference. As he walked back to his apartment, he realized that he couldn't be the same as before. He didn't know what to do with himself. He couldn't live by himself in Little Falls; he couldn't go back to his old life with his old friends. He didn't fit anywhere. He wished he could go to Max with this problem. Max knew exactly what to tell him. Frustrated, he dialed Kate's number. The call went straight to her voice mail. "Hi, Kate, it's Edward. Call me if you get this message. I need your advice."

A few hours later Edward was sitting in his apartment watching television when Kate returned his call. "Hi, Ed, how are you?" Kate asked.

"Hi, thanks for calling me back. I'm good. Actually I'm not so good. I don't know what's the matter with me. I don't fit in anymore."

"I know what you mean," Kate replied. "It's hard for me too. After living in Little Falls for a few years now, I'm trying to adjust to the fast life myself. I've taken a job at a private law office. They like that I have a lot of experience, since the attorney's just starting up his practice. So it's nice to be able to help. By the way, what are you going to do with Sara's letters?"

Edward replied that he hadn't had time to give that serious thought, though he felt obliged to do something constructive. Her question goaded him to respond without much thought, "Well, I guess I can publish them."

Kate was happy to hear that. She asked how he would go about doing that. When he confessed that he hadn't a clue, she promised to go to the bookstore and buy a book on how to publish. When she wondered if he was going to use Sara's name in any way, he told her that he didn't know how to do that, but was committed to giving Sara the credit.

Kate suggested that he write the book from his viewpoint. "You would write as yourself finding the letters, include them verbatim, and describe how they've affected you."

Edward was simultaneously excited and cautious. "That's a great idea, but it's easier said than done. You are going to help me with this, aren't you?"

Kate assured him, "I'm not sure how I can help you write, but I can keep you company during the process. I'm already excited."

As he thought more about it, Edward realized that he had a lot to write about. He needed to think seriously about all the events that had happened right after he lost his job, one by one. He needed to connect all the dots and clarify everything for himself. He took a pen and notebook and asked Kate to tell him what she thought the important points of the story would be.

She started by saying, "Losing your job was probably the best thing that happened to you."

Edward corrected her, "I actually didn't quite lose the job, since I wasn't fired or laid off. I was given an indefinite amount of time for vacation without pay."

Kate smiled. "So you still haven't come to terms with that, am I right?"

Not wanting to argue, Edward just nodded and told her she was probably right. Deep inside his heart he knew that it didn't matter who was right. Nevertheless, he told himself that he was going to let her win only this one time.

Edward was pleased to hear that Kate was going to support him in writing the book. He felt very close to her. They exchanged addresses and agreed to meet at a coffee shop to discuss the project further. When they met later, Edward announced that he planned to write for a living. Kate thought it a wonderful idea, but counseled him to focus on this one first. They discussed how Max had to play a central role, along with Edward's dreams. They agreed to include Lady, the gigantic tree. Edward grew almost giddy. "What should we name this book?"

"Wait until it is finished and name it later," Kate responded.

"Are you sure you don't want to be a co-author?" Edward asked.

"No thanks, Ed, I don't want the responsibility. You can thank me in the book if you want. But please don't scare me away by asking me to write." He promised to thank her in the beginning of the book.

Writing full-time affected Edward positively, making him realize how he had reached his present state in life. He had to remember his conversations with Max and Kate in detail, which led him to understand how his deep friendship with Max had been so constructive for him. He spent the first three days just thinking about the past events and outlining all the important points that he could recall.

Then he began to write.

CHAPTER FOURTEEN

Edward spent the next three months writing. His first page consumed a week. He pondered over the process of putting thoughts onto a page and then organizing them so they came alive, so the reader felt events as he had. He discovered how hard it was to create a story that compelled the reader to want more. He increasingly yearned to express his whole heart and soul. This was his chance. He had to do it for himself. He also had to write for Max and Sara and Kate. He knew that his mother was somewhere watching him. He knew that a lot of little angels were happy for him and one special angel was content because of him. While writing late one night, he was so exhausted that he fell asleep at his laptop and began dreaming one of his vivid dreams.

He sat before his laptop writing when he suddenly noticed his little angel playing with the keyboard. *Please, little guy, be careful. I am writing our story*, Edward thought. Just like before, he could hear his own voice inside his chest.

The angel looked at him. "Edward Evans, I am ready to show you to the door again." As Edward looked up, he saw the golden door standing tall in the middle of the room. Walking up to it, he asked the little angel what was behind it. The angel instructed him to open the door and receive what was promised him. Edward wasn't sure what the little angel meant. Placing his hand on the knob, he opened the door very gently, exposing the same narrow wooden bridge of his previous dream, sitting on top of green grass. He stepped onto it and found himself surrounded by bright light. The sky above was a blue shade he had never seen before. After no more than one minute of walking, he came upon a small house with a beige door. To its left was a door bell, which he rang.

An old woman, whom he did not recognize and who looked to be in her eighties, opened the door. She was wearing a blue velvet jacket with a white shirt and a long blue skirt. Greeting him with a big smile, she invited him in. As he entered, he could see that the inside of the house was very well lit. He walked into an open space with old-fashioned furniture. She asked him to sit and make himself comfortable. He noted with disappointment that the coffee table didn't have any of his mother's cookies. The old woman came back and sat on the easy chair across from him. "How are you doing, Edward?" she asked.

"I'm fine, thank you. I'm sorry, but I don't know you."

Smiling warmly, she informed him, "I'm your grandmother. Your father, Jake, is my son."

It had never occurred to Edward that he might meet his grandmother. She looked like a very sweet lady. He didn't know what to say to her. He'd felt connected with her all along, but didn't understand why.

"You'll be excited to learn that you're going to see Jake. He's happy to see you and will be here soon," his grandmother informed him. Edward could hear his heart beating. He couldn't believe he was going to see his father after so many years. He kept smiling at this sweet old woman. After a few minutes, she told him that she was going to leave. She walked up to him and kissed the top of his head, which made him feel even more deeply connected to her. He didn't want her to leave, but she withdrew very slowly out of the room without saying good-bye.

While Edward sat on the couch, he tried to imagine what he would ask his father when they saw each other. He was deep in his thoughts when he felt a warm, strong hand on his right shoulder. He turned back and saw that his father was standing behind him, smiling. "Edward, my boy, I'm so glad to see you."

Edward stood up, turned toward his father, and gave him a big hug. "Dad, I've missed you so much," Edward whispered into his father's ear as he held him in his arms. They continued holding each other for a long time in silence. Edward didn't want to say anything. When he was a young boy helping his father do a job, his dad never talked much and Edward loved being quiet with him. As the two men silently continued to hold each other, Edward suddenly realized that he could physically feel the love that his dad had for him, a deep flow of emotion that he had never experienced. Pure love was circling their bodies. It was wonderful. His eyes closed, a rush of memories filled his heart and mind. One by one he saw his childhood memories with his father flashing before him and could feel what his father felt for him. He felt amazing amounts of love and acceptance pouring into him, over-flowing his being. Edward had never realized how much his father, not given to many words, loved him.

When they finally separated, Edward asked him, "Why didn't you ever tell me how you felt about me? I never knew how much you really loved me."

His father confessed, "I didn't know how to tell you without being vulnerable to you. When we're vulnerable, we're so easily hurt." Edward couldn't believe how real his experience felt. He knew that there weren't enough words to explain it. He looked at his father's face and for the first time saw a man who was distinct from him. They weren't connected as Edward used to imagine, assuming everyone had only Edward's point of view. He had just learned how to really love, by watching his father love him.

Edward knew that his time was up and he had to go back to his life. He wasn't sure why he was being given this opportunity to see this other level of existence. He couldn't believe that he was that special. His father turned around and walked out of the room without turning back. Edward sat back on the couch and tried to remember every detail of what he was experiencing. Suddenly his grandmother stood smiling before him. Edward asked her why he was seeing people who had died and passed on with the faces they had when he knew them. She told him that the images were only from his experience, that the energy of our loved ones will manifest to us as we remember them. Edward got up and walked toward the entry door. As he exited, he said his good-byes in his heart to his father and his newly found grandmother. He walked over the wooden bridge until he reached the golden door. He turned the door knob and stepped back into his apartment.

The next day Edward woke up to Kate's knock on the door. When he opened the door for her, she walked excitedly into the apartment and told him she had great news. She'd talked to a friend she knew and trusted in the publishing business, and she wanted him to finish the book as soon as possible so they could send it to her friend for publishing. Edward wasn't sure if he understood. "What do you mean? They're going to publish the book? Who are they?"

"My friend didn't promise to publish the book for sure, but she's an editor who works with some of the biggest publishers, and she's going to take a look at your book. I just know it'll be great and will be published," Kate said encouragingly. Edward agreed to work on his finishing touches. He thanked Kate for having so much faith in him, but he warned her not to get her hopes too high.

The following week, Edward and Kate sat in their favorite coffee shop, sipping coffee and discussing a good title for the book. "What about *Sara's Letters?*" Edward ventured.

"No, that sounds too vague," Kate countered.

"What about *The Circle of Life,*" Edward asked. "meaning that you have to live your life fully to understand the purpose and meaning of it?"

"I'm not sure about that," Kate answered, "it's too generic. Anyway, I think Disney has a copyright on that one…hee hee."

"What about *An Extraordinary Day,*" Edward continued, "referring to the day I lost my job and fiancée, leading me on a path of self-discovery?"

Kate noted that the phrase could apply to Edward's meeting Max for the first time, or even coming upon the tree called Lady, or finding Sara's letters. Pausing briefly, she then excitedly cried out, "What about *The Sacred Porch?*"

"That's it! I really like that!" Edward exploded in celebration. "You're right. Everything happened around that porch. It brought me to work for Max. It hid Sara's papers, which got me thinking about what I really wanted from life, prompted Max to bring you over for readings, and inspired the two of us to work together on this book. We'll call it *The Sacred Porch*."

Several weeks passed after Edward submitted his book to Kate's friend for editing. One evening while Edward sat in his apartment reading some news on the Internet, his cell phone rang. The voice on the other end of the line was someone from the editor's office with good news. A publisher was interested in his book and wanted to meet with him to go over the details. He thanked the woman and eagerly wrote down the contact number. He called Kate to tell her the great news and invite her out that evening to celebrate. They dined at a local restaurant that Kate selected, reserving a table for four so as to include Max and Sara. They knew this gesture made no difference to Max and Sara, but it was immensely important to them.

Edward was living his dream. He had written about what had changed his life's path, a book that explained the change to himself and hopefully would stimulate change for others. He was a different man. He was doing what he had always been afraid to do—write. He continuously reflected on how Sara's letters were profoundly changing his life almost daily. He had to believe in a force greater than him that pulled him to Little Falls and that dilapidated porch, that prompted Max to hire Edward, and that inspired Sara to write. He felt connected to Sara. *The Sacred Porch* was inspired by and completed her work.

Edward was deeply gratified that he had Kate to share his happiness. With Max gone, she alone understood what had happened to him and what he continued to go through. Indeed, she had pushed him many times to get him to this point. He didn't have to explain himself to her, and he could count on her support. He was truly blessed. As they dined together, he talked about his experience at his old job with an insurance company: how he would go to work with no passion just to fit in with society's expectations of him. She had no trouble understanding what he was talking about. They concluded the evening by expressing how they missed Max and wished that he had been there to share their joy.

On his way home, Edward thought about where Max might be. Was he somewhere in space? Could he actually see Edward? Or hear him? Edward couldn't be sure of anything. His vivid dreams suggested more to life than what we're normally aware of, but he didn't have any concrete answers. He thought about Sara's faith. Sara knew in her heart that her letters reached God. Where did her clear knowing come from? Edward had this indescribably strong connection to her that he wished he understood. Would that he knew her in person. Perhaps she could enlighten him about it.

Several months passed before *The Sacred Porch* was published. Its success overwhelmed and exhausted him. To get away from the enthusiastic crowds, he decided to spend some time at Max's old house. Driving there, he recalled his first trip a year ago and wondered at his transformation since then. He reached the house in a few hours. After parking in the driveway, he remained in the car observing the scene. It had kept its quiet serenity even while the house continued to fall apart. The decline was buffered by the beautiful tall trees surrounding it as well as the fresh scent from the new wood of the porch. He had an idea. He called Kate. "Hello, Kate, it's me."

"Hi, Edward, what's going on?"

He explained excitedly, "I'm here at Max's house...our house...I want to rebuild the whole house piece by piece...to give the porch a nice home."

Intrigued, Kate inquired, "What are you saying?"

Edward explained, "Max and the porch gave me…gave us…a new life. They also gave us a house, which is a kind of a symbol of that new life. I can't let what they gave us gradually turn into rubble. Termites have destroyed so much of the wood that repair is useless. If we want to keep it, then we should rebuild it."

Moved by his feeling for the place, Kate responded warmly, "That's such a beautiful thought, Edward. I'd love to help you with it, but I can't leave my job. How are you going to do it alone?"

Edward assured her, "Don't worry, this'll be good for me. I need the exercise."

"What about the expenses?" Kate asked. "I don't have extra money to pay for my share."

He told her not to worry about that. He only needed her permission, since they owned the house together. Kate thanked him for his thoughtfulness. She assured him that she appreciated all of his hard work and would help him with the rebuilding on weekends when she could. When they hung up, Edward returned to the house for his toolbox. Max had left plenty of brand new wood, probably knowing at some level that Edward would eventually save the house.

Though Edward felt overwhelmed by the amount of work that he was taking on, he was braced by his need to do some physical work that would keep him busy. He began with the north living room wall, which looked especially damp. While removing one section to explore any damage underneath, he kept thinking about Kate. Did she have special feelings for him? If she did, why had she never said or done anything to him that suggested it? She was always busy and now had a job in a law firm that took even more of her time. He could see that she cared about him; she had been extremely supportive while he wrote his book and instrumental in getting it published. On the other hand, he hadn't raised the subject with her either, though he had strong feelings for her that he could no longer ignore. Then it hit him. Lily had approached him first. She was the one who took their relationship to the next level. Even though he was the one who proposed to her, she had already made it clear that she wanted to marry him. There was no risk that she would reject him. Looking back on his life, he could now see that he'd never initiated anything where he faced rejection. Maybe Lily had been right. Maybe he was intimidated by his boss's rejection. Maybe he could have been more assertive. He needed a friend to talk to, but couldn't think of anyone with whom he could dare reveal how vulnerable he felt about this. After meeting Lily, he had spent less and less time with his old friends, whom she had not taken to. And after his transformation in Little Falls, he found that he no longer connected with them at all.

After removing the sheetrock, Edward drove to the hardware store for materials to complete the job. It took him three days to replace the north living room wall sheetrock, leaving him satisfied with the quality of his work and the time it had taken. Taking a break on the porch for some water, he thought about Aunt Mary, with whom he'd been especially close as a child. Actually, she was his father's aunt, Edward's late grandmother's sister. She was in her eighties and lived by herself. He winced when he realized that he hadn't called her for years. He recalled how kind she had been to him and how she had encouraged him to read good books to help him become the good writer he wanted to be. It had been so long since he'd called her that he no longer had her number. Though it took information less than a minute to give him her number, he wondered if it was still hers and not someone else's with the same name. He dialed the number with little hope, but after three rings Aunt Mary picked up the phone.

"Hello?"

"Hello, Aunt Mary? This is Edward. Do you remember me?"

"Hello, Eddie, of course I remember you. I have many of your pictures with me. How are you? I'm so happy to hear your voice. What are you up to these days?"

Edward didn't know what to say. He knew that he needed to connect with someone who cared. And was wise. His parents had greatly respected her. A retired school teacher, she was always reading something in her free time.

"Do you still read a lot of books, Aunt Mary?"

"Of course, Eddie. You know I never stop. It's harder for me to read now; my eyes aren't as sharp as they used to be. But I still manage, you know. I have to, so I can keep up with the times."

Edward was excited to share his news with her. "Aunt Mary, I've written a book that you might be interested in." That was all Edward had to say for her to insist he come to her house the following day. She commanded him to bring her a new copy of his book and spend the whole day with her. She would cook him something special for lunch. Edward said to himself that thinking of her had been an inspiration.

Since Edward kept copies of his book in the trunk of his car and kept clothing at the old house, he spent the night there rather than return to his apartment. He would leave early in the morning to drive to his aunt's. The house was calm and peaceful as he climbed the stairs to his room for the night. When he lay down on the bed, his eyes quickly became heavy and he began to dream.

Edward was floating outside his body, watching himself from above. He could not speak, only observe. Facing a wall made up of large rocks that he needed to remove, he was trying to choose which one to start with. He experienced the decision process as strangely non-physical. Behind the wall he could see clouds of energy but could not feel the energy itself. As he witnessed his body turn to remove the chosen rock from the wall, he noticed that the visible but unfelt cloud of energy was blocking the rock from being moved. He wanted desperately to tell his body not to waste its energy trying, but he couldn't communicate with it. When his body eventually got tired of trying, Edward chose another rock. When his body turned to remove that one, the cloud of energy placed itself on the other side of the wall to help. When he saw that, Edward knew that his body was going to succeed. He watched in awe at how easy it now was for his body to remove the large rock from the wall. So while floating above himself, Edward saw how this cloud of energy blocked his body from removing one rock and helped his body move another. Yet at the same time, Edward believed that he was the one who accomplished the task of removing the rock and took great pride in doing so, since he was the one who chose the task in the first place.

He immediately recognized that this was a lesson in the different roles that free will and destiny play in human choices. He saw how he could make his own choices about what to accomplish in the physical world, but how there was also an invisible force that either blocked or assisted him in accomplishing them. Free will worked hand in hand with this force. Free will was necessary, since choices were needed to select from many possible goals and to move toward accomplishing them. Each of us has to decide what's worth doing, then our body must put energy and time into achieving it. Planning is a crucial and necessary component of achieving anything, but the plan has to align with the invisible force that is working for that individual.

Edward flowed in understanding. He swam in the vast knowledge of how his life truly made sense. He saw what Sara meant by saying that there was a force that had pushed him to take the job with Max. That force had helped all those in his story do what they freely chose to do. The path that he had chosen must therefore have been the right path for him. In the future, there would be many different paths that would reach the destination toward which the force pushed him. If he listened to his heart and stopped being afraid of failure, that invisible force would assist him. Whenever he listened to his intuition, he would be allowing the invisible force to carry him to his destination. He still had to put energy into reaching his goals, but when he was on the right path of following his intuition, the invisible force of the universe would assist him every step of the way like a lingering voice within that kept giving him hints.

Unfortunately, alongside the inner voice of intuition existed that of blind impulse, which assumed the cloak of wisdom but sometimes compelled him to seek short-term gain at the price of what was really worthwhile. Edward realized that he had often confused impulse with intuition and that he sometimes needed his reasoning mind to help him tell the difference. In short, his life was a constant dialogue between reasoning and intuition, each educating but sometimes misleading the other in its own way. At first bewildered by this insight, Edward was tempted to despair of ever finding a reliable guide that he could trust. However, when he reflected on his whole life's path, Edward realized that whenever he had approached a challenge with an open heart his intuition had dominated, in the long run correcting any mistakes made from following impulse—making the continual dialogue between reasoning and intuition a self-correcting one.

Edward now deeply understood that his life had a great purpose within which there were many smaller ones. Some of those smaller purposes served the great one, but others did not. So he all too often made mistaken choices, which sometimes made him afraid of making any choice at all. However, he now understood how even when a chosen path failed and made him feel bad, his true essence had been there to catch him, making him feel safe enough to learn from his mistake and move forward.

While he digested these deeply nourishing thoughts, Edward kept floating in the sky, getting further away from his physical body. Though he was ascending into mysterious dimensions that he had never experienced or whose existence he had never even suspected, he had no fear. As he floated higher to new energy fields, he saw colors he had never seen before and could find no words to describe. The understanding that was flowing into his consciousness was so overwhelmingly vast that he couldn't imagine how his physical body could ever digest it. All his previous dreams seemed to have been preparing him for this one. The invisible life force was connecting him to all life, making him one with everyone. The same force that grows flowers and from which everything in the universe flows had also impelled him to take Max's remodeling job. He could see that the closer life got to its natural state, the better the life force flowed through it. He saw how growth in technology and speeding up the natural processes of life could be either part of the life force or obstruct it, depending on our choices.

As Edward floated still higher into the different energy fields, he understood how everything, including his physical body, was just vibration. Until now, he had understood this through the laws of physics, but now he felt it intuitively, just as in previous dreams he had heard loving voices—his own and others'—from within. Everything was continuously moving and changing vibrations of energy, with one's experience depending on a vibration's speed and wavelength. Because he was one with all energy, he understood that a vast consciousness was blending within his own, feeding him this knowledge. He was unaware of time or space, only of the vibrating flow and his realization that everything was meant to be learned and understood. At the core of everything was only one feeling, love. Everything else was derivative: born of love.

He began to descend back toward his physical body, which he could see was vibrating at a very weak pace. As he approached, he saw a field of energy that surrounded his physical body but was itself not physical. With his mind, he could see the field very clearly and understood that the field's vibration would change every time the physical body's did. Everything was connected. As he began to re-enter his body fully, he was unsure of how much of this dream he might remember, but he was certain that he would never be the same.

CHAPTER FIFTEEN

Edward woke up with a new level of energy. He remembered his dream vividly, the source of his new realization that he wasn't alone. He was part of a great purpose, which gave him a trust in himself that enabled him to live his life fully.

He showered, shaved, and changed to more formal clothing for his visit with Aunt Mary. As he drove to her house, he thought of the times they had shared together and all the stories his father would tell about her. He wondered what she would say when she read his book. After three hours on the road, he parked in front of her small one-level beige house. The front yard was green grass surrounded by the proverbial white picket fence. On the front porch were three rows of decorative pots filled with a variety of flowers, which made the scene uniquely colorful.

When Edward rang the bell, Aunt Mary opened the door after the briefest of pauses. Like his grandmother, she was in her eighties. She was small-framed and thin, her white hair neatly pulled back from her face. She wore a pink long-sleeved blouse and a white long summer skirt that covered her feet. He was pleased that he had decided to see her. He had so much to tell her. She was going to be so proud of him for what he had done. She greeted him with a smile and gave him a big hug.

Taking his hand and leading him inside, she began, "Eddie dear, you finally decided to visit me. I'm so glad you could come. I don't know how you could find time in your young life to visit your father's old aunt. I really miss your father. He was such a great man. You actually look like him now. Do you see that yourself?"

"Actually, no I don't, Aunt Mary. Apparently it's easier for others to see the resemblance, because I just don't see it. But it makes me happy that you say it. My mom used to say that my dad was very handsome in his younger days."

"Of course he was," Aunt Mary confirmed, showing Edward to the family room couch. He sat down and looked around. Everything was placed in perfect color combination. All her crystal antiques stood on a coffee table to the side of the couch. Several blue and white picture frames holding family pictures were on a side table across from where Edward was sitting.

The wall next to the window had a wooden shelf filled with books. He remembered how Aunt Mary loved stories. "Well, Aunt Mary, I'm not going to tell you the story. It would ruin the book for you. But I am going to tell you that everything I wrote is true. It all happened to me. I can't wait for you to read it so we can discuss it together. I hope you'll like it." Edward was anxious for his aunt Mary to read his book, since he cared about her opinion. He had always thought of her as being a very wise woman, since his parents used to go to her with their problems. Aunt Mary always knew what to say to make them feel better. She had a simple, practical way of seeing everything. Smiling, she replied, "Well, where is this book of yours, Eddie? I'll read it right away. I'm glad my eyes are still working."

Edward took a copy out of his laptop bag and gave it to her. "Well…*The Sacred Porch*…that's certainly an interesting title. I'm very curious," she assured him. She placed the book on her coffee table and asked him if he was hungry for lunch.

Edward hadn't had a meal this good for a long time. Aunt Mary had prepared her special lasagna for him, its taste taking him back to his childhood. She had always made it when Edward and his parents visited her. He missed having them here.

"Eddie dear, do you have a special someone in your life yet?" Aunt Mary asked abruptly.

Edward smiled. "Well, I'm not sure if I have her in my life. I do have her on my mind."

Aunt Mary laughed agreeably. "That's a good start. For someone to be in your life, you first need them on your mind. I guess that's the way things come about, don't you think?"

"I know, but this is little complicated. I'm not sure how she feels about me. She doesn't give me any hints. I'm not sure if she only wants to be my friend or she thinks of me as more than that."

"So what's this young lady's name?" Aunt Mary asked.

"Kate," he explained. "We're pretty close. We met when I had just broken up with someone else, so I'm not sure how she's thinking of me. I was very unsure of myself when we first met. I've grown a lot since, but I'm not sure if it's enough to impress her."

"Don't be so sure, Edward. Do you know how your parents met?" Aunt Mary offered.

"No, I don't. I just assumed that they knew each other from high school," he confessed.

"Yes, they did," she continued. "They went to the same high school. But your father liked your mother for two years before he got the courage to ask her out. My sister, your grandmother Ruth, used to tell me about it. Jake used to tell Ruth how he didn't think that your mother would like him. Well, the rest is history. You never know until you ask. Anyway, Eddie, if something is meant to be, then it will be. Don't you believe that?"

Edward's mind took him back to his latest dream. He knew exactly what his aunt was talking about. He remembered realizing that if something was part of his life purpose—his so-called destiny—the life force or energy would help carry him toward that goal. Just as Aunt Mary said, if it was meant to be, it would be. Only he was afraid to face the disappointment if it wasn't meant to be with Kate. He was going to be really hurt if he found out they had different destinies. This was not what he had faced with Lily. Their relationship wasn't the same as his and Kate's. In Kate, Edward had found a friend he could count on. He respected her opinion on things, whereas Lily seemed to be in her own world. They didn't seem to share the same goals. She needed him only to fill an empty place in her life, so that he felt replaceable even when they were together. Kate, on the other hand, related to others very personally. She had found a friend and mentor in Max and stood by him until the end. Edward respected that in her. It was not only admirable; it evoked in him a sense of safety.

Edward was grateful that he had someone like Aunt Mary to talk to. He wondered out loud, "Aunt Mary, how come you didn't get married?"

Not surprisingly, she replied forthrightly. "Edward, I wasn't always so wise as I am now. When I was in my late teens, I cared for a man who was about fifteen years older than I was. He traveled a lot and asked me to wait for him. I believed him, so I waited. He would see me once in a while, but he always had an excuse about not having enough money to start a family or not having enough time to stay around. He always said that his job was very demanding and he had to wait until he got promoted. I believed him. I should say that I wanted to believe him. My parents and my sister Ruth told me not to. They advised me to go after my own life, but I didn't listen. Well, I finally stopped waiting, but only after I heard from a trustworthy source that he had his own family in another part of the country. He had lied to me. I was crushed. I didn't want to believe the truth. You see, Ed, truth has a way of getting in your face until you believe it. I got over him. I loved books, so I kept myself busy going to school, teaching little children, and reading more books. I don't know what happened to the years. I just got lost in my work with children and at home in my books."

Edward was impressed. Unable to imagine his fragile old aunt as a young woman, he asked if she had a picture from those days. When she left the family room in search of one, he congratulated himself on his good fortune to have her as a relative. The thought shamed him for having ignored her for so long a time. Why hadn't he visited her before? He should have come to her when he got engaged to Lily. Or before. She was a gracious person who didn't hold anything against him, but accepted him as young and busy. However, he now knew better, having learned how fragile life is— how easy it is to have someone around in one moment and not there the next. He still couldn't believe that Max had died so suddenly and that he got to be there with him on his last day.

Aunt Mary came back to the family room with three black-and-white pictures. She handed them to a disbelieving Edward. Was this really Aunt Mary? The first picture was of a girl about seventeen or eighteen years old with a ponytail, standing in the middle of a football field. She wore a long dark skirt and a light-colored top. She had a beautiful smile showing pearl-white teeth. The next picture was a radiant young woman in her twenties holding a book and standing in the center of three young children around seven years of age. The last picture was a close-up of her in the second one. She wore a sun hat and had on dark lipstick and makeup. She was really beautiful.

Edward was moved. "You are so amazing in these pictures, Aunt Mary. Thank you for sharing them with me. I'm so honored."

"Of course, Edward, I have a lot of fun showing them myself. I usually don't have too much company anymore. For one thing, I like to stay alone, but also it's hard to find friends my age, since not many of them are up to socializing. But I like my life. I think I'm doing what I came here to do. Sometimes I have regrets that I didn't marry and have children of my own, but then who knows if that would have left me as happy as I am now? As the philosopher Santayana famously said, 'History doesn't reveal its alternatives.' Anyway, I sure am glad that Jake got married to your mother and now I have you to share all of this with." She walked up to Edward and kissed him on his head. He sat quietly, enjoying their being together.

Late that afternoon, Edward thanked Aunt Mary and told her to call him when she finished the book because he was dying to know what she thought about it. Making sure to write his phone number in her notebook, she promised to call and tell him her honest opinion, though she assured him she couldn't imagine she wouldn't be thrilled with it.

Later that night in his apartment he thought about her life, deciding he would sit down with her and invite her to tell him everything that she wanted people to know about herself so he could write her life story.

Since the next day was Saturday, Edward called Kate to see if she was free to spend some time together. When she didn't answer, he left a message then showered, dressed, and headed out for a walk and a strong cup of coffee. As he stepped out of his apartment, he spied the young boy who had sold him the newspaper and homemade cookie on the day he read the ad from Max. He excitedly yelled for the boy to come over. The boy walked slowly toward him with a plate full of cookies in one hand and a few newspapers in the other.

"Where do you live?" Edward asked.

"I live on the next block, sir," the boy answered.

"These are amazing cookies, where do you get them?"

"My mom bakes them, sir."

"Does she bake them all the time?" Edward asked.

"Sometimes she does. It helps us with money."

"Well, they're delicious. They remind me of my mother's." The boy stared at Edward puzzled, not knowing if Edward wanted to buy from him or just talk. "I'm going to buy all these cookies if you promise to tell your mother that I might be able to help her. The local café where I get my coffee could use delicious cookies like these. I'd like to introduce your mom to Gary, the owner, who's a very nice guy. You never know." Edward gave the boy a twenty, which seemed a fair price.

"Thank you very much, sir. My name's Mike. I'll tell my mom." The boy quickly ran out of the apartment building.

Edward was determined to help that boy and his family. Knowing how his path had crossed with little Mike's that momentous day made him feel a special connection that compelled him to go out of his way to help the boy and his family. Maybe the desire to help little Mike came from the universal energy that had placed the boy in front of Edward's apartment in the first place. All he knew for sure was that he was going to listen to his intuition if he felt it. He didn't have to understand it. If it was positive and it felt right, it had to be followed. As he was reflecting on all this, he could imagine how Max might be present and proud of him. In any case, it didn't matter if Max really knew what Edward was doing. He himself was proud of what he had become.

Edward opened his apartment door, went directly to his kitchen, grabbed a Ziploc bag, and placed the cookies inside. He would take them to the coffee shop himself and share them with Gary. What could it hurt? If it was meant to be, it would be easy. He would have the force help him. As he walked toward the café, he came across Lily walking by.

"Hi, Edward. Where are you headed?" Lily asked in an upbeat voice.

"Hi, I'm walking to the corner coffee shop."

"If you don't mind, I'll walk with you. I can use some good coffee myself," Lily suggested. Edward didn't say anything. He gave her a stiff smile and continued walking. She came up alongside. "I heard about your book, Edward. Did you write good things about me in it?"

"I didn't ask for your permission, so I didn't use your name. I didn't say anything bad about you, if you're worried about it," Edward informed her.

"I'm not worried, I'm happy for you. All of my complaining eventually worked. You finally did something big. I'm glad that I was hard on you. Don't you agree?" she asked.

He didn't have an answer for her. What meant the most to him at that moment was that he didn't feel weak when he saw her. He wasn't worried about what she thought of him. She didn't have her hooks in him anymore. How fortunate that they'd run into each other. His reaction showed that he was completely over her. Finally he was a free man.

As they reached the coffee shop, Edward held the door open for her. She entered and sat herself at one of the tables by a window. Edward went right to the counter to order his coffee and talk to Gary, who had his usual smile. He was about fifty-five years old, a widower who had lost his wife to cancer. He had two daughters who had gone away to college. He lived alone, content with his coffee shop. "Good morning, Gary. Do you have a minute?" Edward asked.

"For you, Edward, I have more than a minute. What can I do for my best customer?"

Edward replied, "I have these homemade cookies that are out-of-this-world good. They remind me of my mother's. Taste one." Edward opened his Ziploc bag so Gary could take one.

When Gary bit into it, he smiled appreciatively. "Wow, they're way better than what my mother could ever do, God bless her soul. Are you taking a cookie class?" They laughed.

Edward explained, "No, there's this kid, Mike, who brings them to our building to sell. His mother bakes them. I think she might be willing to bake them for your shop. Give them a try. I'll pay for one day's worth so you just give them away to your customers and see what happens. If the response is good, you can make a deal with Mike's mother. What d'ya say?"

Gary agreed that it was a no-lose proposition for him, but he was curious. "Why are you doing this for them?"

Edward explained, "It's a long story. Her son, Mike, changed my life by selling me a newspaper and a cookie. I want to give something back to them now that I have the chance." Gary told Edward to bring this lady with her cookies whenever he could. He was happy to give her, and himself, a chance at a profitable opportunity.

As Edward ordered his coffee, his cell phone rang. It was Kate. He picked up on the first ring. "Hi, Kate, how are you?"

"Hi, Edward, sorry I didn't hear my phone ring. The ringer must have been off. Do you still want to have lunch today?" Kate asked.

"Of course. I have a lot of interesting things to tell you."

"Great, I can't wait to hear them. I'll meet you in two hours at Big Joe's."

Edward wasn't sure if he wanted to buy Lily coffee, but decided to be a gentleman. After buying two coffees, he walked hers to her table. "Here you go, Lily, some fresh coffee for you," he told her, then started to walk out of the shop.

"Aren't you going to drink your coffee with me?" she asked.

Edward turned around and directly faced her. "Sorry, I have to be somewhere. I never suggested we have coffee together. I'm sorry if you misunderstood. Please, enjoy the coffee." He gave Lily a faint smile and walked out the door.

He felt liberated. He saw that Lily was angry, but that was for her to deal with. He hadn't put her in that situation and was no longer committed to her happiness. Since he had plenty of time before he met Kate, he decided to walk for an hour. Max had introduced him to long walks, which he had never previously thought of as an enjoyable exercise. He had always used his car to take him anywhere. The only place where he had exercised was at the local gym, where he was a member. Now, since Max, he enjoyed walking outside, paying attention to his surroundings. He took particular pleasure in walking among trees and nature. It recalled the serenity of Little Falls.

After the walk, Edward went back to his apartment and changed for lunch. He took particular care dressing since he wanted to look good for Kate. He looked forward to lunch with her so he could tell her about Aunt Mary and his latest dream. He knew she would like hearing about them.

CHAPTER SIXTEEN

Big Joe's was a local restaurant that Edward and Kate had frequented while they were working on *The Sacred Porch.* They liked the food and the quiet atmosphere where they could have privacy and talk. As Edward arrived, Kate was parking her car. She wore a blue-and-white shirt with a long white summer skirt with a blue belt. She looked good. Intent on being gentlemanly toward her, Edward deliberately allowed Kate to enter the restaurant first. The hostess took them to a booth by the window and presented their menus. After they had ordered, Kate jokingly commanded Edward to tell her about what was on his mind. He began with the small rebuilding job he had done, then reported his latest dream in great detail. Later he told her about Aunt Mary and the day he had spent with her. Finally he

mentioned seeing Mike again and talking with Gary about helping Mike's mother.

Kate listened to him quietly. She was a great listener. Only after
he was through did she tell him about her job. The new law firm
was doing well and the attorney really appreciated having her
around with all her experience.

Kate was eager to meet Aunt Mary as soon as possible.
Edward promised that he would arrange it as soon as she finished reading his book so the three of them could discuss it.
Kate informed Edward that Max's attorney had sent her papers
verifying that Max had left them the old house. She had brought
a copy for Edward. He took it and thanked her, commenting on
how much he missed Max. She agreed heartily with the senti-
ment. They continued for some time to discuss their mutual
feelings for him.

They talked for hours. When they left the restaurant, it was almost time for dinner. Kate told Edward that she needed to leave
to do some work she had at home. Edward walked her to her
car, standing at that stop silently until she disappeared from the
parking lot. He regretted having to say good-bye. It would be
nice to be at home with her while she worked. He wanted to tell
her how he felt but wasn't quite ready. He blamed himself for
not being more open with her, but he didn't want to mess things
up. Kate was too important to him.

The following day Edward was doing his laundry when his
doorbell rang. He didn't expect company. He opened the door
to a woman in her forties nervously clutching her handbag. She
wore a soft pink blouse and black pants. She was quite attractive,
with soft makeup on her face and long dark hair that was pulled
back to accentuate her strong features. "How can I help you?"
Edward asked.

"My name is Janet. Mike is my son. You asked for me to come here," she replied shyly.

Edward realized that this was little Mike's mother. He hadn't expected her to be so good looking, since he imagined a cookie baker to be short and fat. He was disappointed in himself for stereotyping. "Of course, please come in." When Edward opened the door wide for her, she hesitated and asked if she could stay outside. Edward realized that she didn't know him well enough and had the right to be cautious. "Sure, we can talk here. Your cookies are delicious. How long have you been baking them?"

"I always made them for Mike, but recently I started to bake them for sale. We stay with my father, who otherwise lives by himself. I'm a single mother, so it's nice to have my father's help with Mike while I can help him with everything else around the house."

"That's nice. Sounds like everyone wins. As for selling cookies, I set you up with Gary for my own reasons. You're under no obligation to me. Over a year ago, Mike sold me a paper with an ad in it that changed my life. It's a long story and doesn't matter. I'd just like to repay the favor if I can. I've already talked with Gary, the owner of the coffee shop, and he loved your cookies. So if you can bring me about five trays of your cookies, I'll pay you for them and let Gary try them in his coffee shop. Would tomorrow morning be too soon?"

By now Janet was smiling and relaxed. "Of course I can. Should I bring them to you here?"

"Yes, that'll be fine. By the way, my name's Edward." They shook hands and Janet left.

The next day Janet rang Edward's doorbell at eight-thirty sharp. He opened the door to the sweet smell of freshly baked cookies. She had placed them neatly in a large box and covered them with aluminum foil. Edward took the cookies and asked her to follow him to Gary's coffee shop. Thought it was only a short walk away, he kept having to resist the urge to open the box and bite into one. When they arrived, Gary was busy with the morning rush of customers. Edward suggested that they wait on the corner until the morning rush was over so they could talk to Gary when he wasn't busy.

"I thought you wanted the customers to try the cookies. We need the morning rush," Janet asserted. Not waiting for him to respond, she took the box out of his hands and fought through the crowd to Gary. When Gary saw Janet, he forgot about his customers and the cookies. He had eyes only for her stunning looks. She smiled at him and asked if he would let her join him behind the counter so she could place her cookies inside his empty glass display. Before he could speak, Gary jumped out of her way.

She carefully opened the glass display, grabbed some paper napkins from the side table, and wiped clean the shelves and inside of the glass. While she was still positioning her cookies for display, a woman in line asked her how much they were. Janet didn't know. Both looked at Gary, who could manage only a flushed face from all the excitement he was feeling. In less than a minute, this woman had bolted into his life and had him hooked. He stammered that the cookies were two dollars each.

Janet instantly snatched a pen and folded piece of paper from her purse, drew "$2," and placed the makeshift sign in front of the display. She then withdrew from behind the counter to join Edward, who stood stunned at how efficiently and un-self-consciously this woman had responded to the situation. Clearly she had followed her intuition. The two of them chose a corner table, sat down, and proceeded to watch the morning rush buy up two-thirds of the cookies.

When the rush was over and Gary was free, he came over and introduced himself to Janet, thanking her for her help and Edward for introducing them. Unable to keep his eyes off of her, he shook her hand and asked if she was interested in working with him permanently for several hours a day. Without hesitating, she informed him, "I have a son in fourth grade, and I can come here after I walk him to school. If you have a kitchen here with a bigger oven than mine at home, I can sure use it for baking the cookies." Gary couldn't have been more delighted. After arranging for her to start the next day, Janet and Edward left.

"This Gary guy is kind of cute. You forgot to tell me that," Janet said in an oddly strained voice.

Edward smiled wryly. "I'm sorry, I didn't realize that he was cute until now." When they separated to return to their homes, she thanked him again, earnestly telling him that she would never forget his generosity. He assured her that he was only too glad that he could help.

As Edward walked the rest of the way home, he reflected on the simple way Janet and Gary had just met. He hadn't given it a thought originally, but he could now see them ending up together. "Nothing's impossible," he smiled to himself.

CHAPTER SEVENTEEN

As he entered his apartment, he saw that a message was waiting for him on his home phone. It was Aunt Mary's voice. "Hello, Edward, I finished *The Sacred Porch*. I have to talk to you in person. Please come by my house. I'm home all week this week. I'll be waiting for you."

Was she impressed? Did she have some corrections for him? He dismissed the latter possibility since the book was already in print. He called Kate to see when she could join him in the visit. Because of her job, weekends were best, so Edward called his aunt to let her know that Kate was dying to meet her and discuss the book and to see if that Saturday after lunchtime would be a good day for her.

Kate came to Edward's apartment from work, since it was on the way to Aunt Mary's house. She had slightly highlighted her hair and had on a little more makeup than usual. She wore a brown silk dress, a white belt, and white sandals. Edward over-so-licitously complimented her on her new hair color, his awkward-ness stemming from his persistent nervousness about revealing his true feelings for her. As they walked to his car, he asked her how her job was going. She replied that she really liked it, espe-cially because her new boss was easygoing and very nice to her. On the road, the topic turned to his aunt.

"What do you think she is going to say about the book?" he asked Kate.

She shrugged her shoulders. "I can't be sure. I don't know her that well. I just know that it's a great book." Edward smiled and thanked her for her support, but he was worried what Aunt Mary would say since he knew her to be very critical.

They arrived at Aunt Mary's house and rang the doorbell. Smiling warmly, she opened the door and welcomed them both to her home. She was especially warm and attentive to Kate be-cause of Edward's feelings toward her. She directed them to the couch in her family room, then left to bring them some lemon-ade. Kate looked around at all the colorful decorations, particu-larly impressed with the framed pictures. Aunt Mary returned with the lemonade, placing the pitcher and two glasses on the coffee table in front of the couch so her guests could help themselves. Then she sat down on the couch across from them.

Aunt Mary broke the silence. "Thanks so much for coming. I'm so happy to see both of you here."

"I'm very glad to meet you too, Aunt Mary," Kate responded. "I've heard so many good things about you."

Edward informed his aunt that he'd already told Kate about her beautiful black-and-white pictures from an unbelievably long time ago. Aunt Mary nodded, commenting that she could close her eyes and see herself back in time. Then she abruptly turned the discussion to Edward's book.

"I'm listening intently, Aunt Mary. Please give me your honest opinion about it. I'm ready for the worst," Edward assured her, smiling wryly.

Smiling right back, the old woman leaned toward him. "I'm going to tell you something that you don't expect, Edward. I cried while reading your book. As you can imagine, it was sad to see your friend Max die so suddenly, but that wasn't the main reason I cried. I cried for the things that I knew while reading the book, but you, the writer, didn't know."

Edward didn't have a clue what Aunt Mary was talking about. He looked at Kate, but she too was puzzled. They both kept quiet, waiting for Aunt Mary to continue. "Eddie dear, did your parents ever tell you who your father's grandparents were?"

"Not really," Edward answered.

"Well, my parents—your father's grandparents—were Helen and Stephen. My mother, Helen, was a beautiful woman—tall, lean, and gorgeous. Ruth, my sister, always wanted to end up looking like our mother." Edward interrupted, asking his aunt the point of all this. She continued, "You need to let me finish, Eddie. Be patient, darling. So as I was saying, my mother's name was Helen and her maiden name was Smith. She had a twin sister named Jane. Jane Smith. Jane married and moved to another state, so I never saw much of her. Anyway, my mother, Helen, and her sister, Jane, grew up in Little Falls. That was their home. Their parents were Paul and Sara Tyler. The Sara who wrote those letters was my grandmother and your father's great-grandmother. This means that Max's house once belonged to your ancestors. Maybe the force that you wrote about meant to show you how powerful and meaningful your life really is."

When Aunt Mary finished talking, she picked up her glass and sipped the lemonade. Edward was stone silent, deeply moved. He had just found out why he had felt such a strong connection with Sara. He tried to remember all the details of his dream about her: her reaction when she first saw him, what she had said to him. His eyes were filled with tears. Kate offered him some Kleenex from a box nearby. Edward took them and wept. He had too many emotions to understand why he was crying. Thankfully he was in the company of the two women who best understood him. Kate moved closer to him, placing her hand on his shoulder. Her intent was not to stop him from crying, but to help him give himself completely over to it.

Everything now made sense to him. He suddenly felt that his circle was complete, with Aunt Mary the last piece of the puzzle. The story that began with him being pulled to the little house with the porch had come full circle here in Aunt Mary's family room. He couldn't have written a better ending to the story himself. How wonderful that God saw him that way. He realized that he was being carried by a higher force that knew a lot more than he did, or even Sara or Max. He didn't have to doubt anymore, because he understood that Sara was right to have had so much faith. It had carried her wish over four generations until it reached him. He was the perfect choice, the chosen one to find Sara's letters. He had to find them and learn from them. He had to grow and change because of them. There was nothing to be afraid of. Everything was going to be just as it was meant to be. He was sure about his faith.

Edward thanked Max and Sara and Beth, Max's wife, in his heart. He thanked his parents, his grandmother, and Helen. He thanked Lady, the gigantic tree of Little Falls. His eyes filled with tears as his heart opened up to so much love and faith. There was no going back. His heart was open. He stood up and thanked Aunt Mary for that priceless information. He understood why he had to be the chosen one. There couldn't have been anyone else who could have done what he did. The universe had the plan all along. By listening to his inner voice, he had opened the way for himself to unravel this great mystery with the letters.

Edward needed space to absorb it all. Rising from the couch, he gave Aunt Mary a big hug and told her that he better leave. Kate also hugged her, thanking her for this gift of an evening, then followed him out. Kate offered to drive, which he gratefully accepted.

When they arrived at his apartment, she asked him if he needed to be alone or wanted company. He begged her to stay. They hung out together in his apartment the rest of the day, just watching television without mentioning anything that had happened. She understood that he needed time to digest everything. Early in the evening, she got up to leave, asking him to call her in the morning so they could discuss everything. There were too many coincidences for them to ignore. Before they heard Aunt Mary's tale, they had been amazed enough about how Edward ended up finding Sara's letters. But after they found out who Sara was, they were awed all the more at the miracle of it all. They knew they were witnesses to something that no one could explain. They would never be the same. Life as they knew it had changed for them right in front of their eyes. They had experienced an extraordinary series of events that had shown them how much meaning their lives had—for Edward, who was the main character in these events, and for Kate, who was brought into them to witness and help him and finally to join him in owning this old house with such a long, personal history.

CHAPTER EIGHTEEN

Edward woke up early in the morning and took a long, warm shower. After dressing, he called Kate to have her meet him at Gary's coffee shop. As he waited for her there, he watched Gary and Janet cheerfully working together. Janet was already clearly in charge. The place looked much cleaner and the customers no longer had to bring their own pastries. Gary couldn't stop smiling. Edward stood up and pulled a chair for Kate when she arrived. She smiled and greeted him warmly. He asked her what she wanted to drink, then got up and brought back their coffees. He wasn't afraid anymore. When she let her right hand rest on the table, he affectionately placed his left hand on it. He spoke softly but confidently. "I need to tell you something that I've wanted to tell you for a long time now, Kate. I need to tell you about my feelings for you. I'm not going to wait any longer."

"I'm here, Edward. I'm listening."

The End

AUTHOR'S NOTE

Dear reader,

I wrote *The Scared Porch* as I channeled it, while I was in a most beautifully elevated state free from worry and doubt, a magical trusting space full of wonder and joy. My deepest prayer is for you to experience *The Sacred Porch* as I did and see your own journey to be as extraordinary as it truly is. May God bless your every moment.

I want to thank my wonderful husband, Shahin, to whom I am dedicating this book. I am also very grateful to my friend Francesca Schaper for her help in rough editing, my editor Gary Schouborg for his excellent final editing, and the bestselling author Ali Pervez who helped with the marketing of this book.

With Love,
Azita

CPSIA information can be obtained at www.ICGtesting.com
Printed in the USA
LVOW04s1458180615

442982LV00018B/903/P